SIXTH INNING
IN
SOUTHAVEN

by
Phil Hardwick

QUAIL RIDGE PRESS
Brandon, Mississippi

Printed in Canada

On the cover: Snowden Grove Park
Photo courtesy of Southaven Chamber of Commerce

Other books in Phil Hardwick's Mississippi Mysteries Series:

Captured in Canton
Collision in Columbia
Conspiracy in Corinth
Cover-Up in Columbus
Found in Flora
Justice in Jackson
Newcomer in New Albany
Vengeance in Vicksburg

To request more information about the Mississippi Mysteries
Series, please send your name and complete mailing address to:

QUAIL RIDGE PRESS
P. O. Box 123 • Brandon, MS 39043
1-800-343-1583 • www.quailridge.com

or visit the author's website at
www.philhardwick.com

ACKNOWLEDGMENTS

The author is grateful to the following persons who provided assistance, advice and encouragement in the creation of this book.

George Dale

Diane Hill

Wayne Hissong

Jon Reeves

Board of Directors of the Southaven
Chamber of Commerce/Main Street

Anonymous citizens of Southaven

Staff of Quail Ridge Press

• • •

Readers who would like more information about Southaven, Mississippi may wish to contact the Southaven Chamber of Commerce/Main Street office at 1-800-272-6551 or on the World Wide Web at www.southavenchamber.com.

CHAPTER 1

Jack Boulder, Mississippi's premier private investigator, woke up nervous on the last Wednesday morning in June.

Although he had over twenty years of law enforcement service and several years thereafter of private detective work, he did not feel just right that day. His maternal aunt would say that he was "beside himself." During his career, he had faced guns, hostile people, angry judges, devious co-workers and conniving lawyers. For some reason, all of that seemed so tame and mild compared to what he was facing today.

Andrew Jackson Boulder put on shorts, a St. Louis Cardinals T-shirt, running shoes and socks. He spent a few minutes stretching his muscles, mostly his hamstrings, then headed out of his downtown Jackson condominium for his morning jog, a mile and a half venture up North State Street to Millsaps College and back. When he returned he discovered his nosy, but dignified, neighbor, retired Navy Admiral Charles Brovard, in the brick courtyard of the complex.

"You look like you just took a shower," the Admiral said. "Bet the humidity is already over ninety percent."

"I wouldn't disagree," Boulder said, still huffing and puffing.

"Are you going to do the deed today?"

"Yes sir. I think today's the day."

"Where is it going to take place?"

"At the University Club," Boulder said.

The University Club is downtown Jackson's private establishment where the Who's Who in the Capital City meet and greet and usually dine. It occupies the top floor of the tallest downtown building, an edifice that is subject to having its name changed after each bank merger. The waitstaff at the club take great care to call the members by name and an award-winning chef runs the kitchen. The furnishings are clubby and the view is as spectacular as one can get in a city that is sited on gently rolling hills at 365 feet above sea level. It is exactly the kind of place that Jack Boulder stays away from.

"Good choice, my boy," the Admiral said. "I took Irma there for dinner last month for our anniversary. Do you think the other party has any suspicion of what's about to take place?"

"I don't think so."

"I didn't know you were a member there."

"I'm not," Boulder said. "But Laura is. Today is her birthday and I told her I wanted to take her to lunch. She said that she was too busy to leave the building, so we're going to the University Club on her membership."

"Good planning, if I say so myself."

"Along with some good luck," Boulder said.

Boulder went inside his condo, took a shower, dressed and then watched the morning news shows. At 9:00 a.m. he called the head of loss prevention at one of his insurance company clients. They discussed an out-standing case involving a worker who had filed an allegedly fraudulent claim. The company had received information that the insured was installing a swimming pool in his back yard, and doing a lot of the excavation work himself. Could Boulder obtain photographic evidence? Boulder assured his client that he would begin staking out the man tomorrow. He made two more calls to clients and advised them of the status of their cases.

At 11:00 a.m. he put on his navy blue suit. It was the only suit he owned and it was used mostly for funerals and weddings. Last year he used it twice, both for funerals of fathers of old friends. He needed to wear it today because a coat and tie are required of gentlemen in the fine dining room of the University Club. While tying the red and blue striped necktie, he noticed his hands were slightly trembling. He clipped his pager on his belt and made a mental note that he needed to break down and buy a cell phone. The things annoyed him because people had become so discourteous with their use of the little communication devices. He and Laura had noticed that the last four times they had eaten out at a restaurant someone had interrupted their conversation to talk on a cell phone. The little vibrating pager was so much more respectful.

At 11:45 a.m. he left his residence and walked across Smith Park to his target building, got on the elevator and punched the button that read "University Club." On his way up, he felt his ears pop slightly and his stomach become queasy. This mission was not going to be easy.

The elevator door opened and Laura Webster, his high school sweetheart of twenty-five years ago, greeted him with a smile.

"Jack," Laura said with a smile. "How nice of you to suggest this place for lunch today. I'm so busy I wouldn't have had time to leave the building to go anywhere else. And you look so good in a coat and tie."

Laura is a partner at one of the big law firms in the same building. The firm occupies two whole floors below.

They walked around to the main dining room and Laura gave her membership number to the maitre de who greeted her by name. At noon they were seated. A white cloth napkin was laid on his lap. He smiled across at his luncheon companion. A tall waiter efficiently presented each of them with a large menu, then said, "Hello, Miss Webster, I'm Fred and I'll be serving you today." Fred told them about the specials of the day and the couple nodded. Fred said that he would be back after they had decided.

"Happy Birthday," Boulder said.

"Thank you," she replied.

Holding up a glass of ice water in toast to her, he said, "Here's a happy birthday wish to someone who looks younger than she did five years ago." He meant it. She was getting better looking all the time. Classier, more professional, every day.

"Thank you," Laura said.

"Busy day?"

"Like all of them," she replied with an exhaling breath. "I've got a pre-trial conference this afternoon. If we can't settle the case, we go to trial tomorrow morning. That's why I couldn't guarantee dinner tonight, I might be unavailable until who knows when."

"I understand."

"What's going on in the private detective world?" she asked.

"Not too much," he said. "This afternoon I've got to take some photos of some vacant lots. A mortgage lender in Virginia made a loan on some Mississippi subdivision property and suspects that there might be fraud involved. Seems like the loans were packaged and sold as if there were houses and buyers there. Unfortunately for the lender, I drove by and could find neither."

"Sounds like an interesting case."

"It has potential," he said.

Fred the server returned and took their orders. Boulder took another sip of water. His stomach tightened as he prepared to pop the question. After his first marriage he swore one night in a bar in front of four St. Louis police detectives that he would never get married again, but here he was, about to make the commitment. If there was a right woman for him Laura was the one. He reached down in his pocket and removed the small, black felt-covered box.

"I got you something small for your birthday this year," he said and handed the box to her.

She smiled coyly and said, "Hmm, what's this?"

He almost said that it wasn't earrings, but just smiled and kept his mouth shut waiting for the ritual to play itself out. She opened it slowly, turning her head slightly as she did so and smiled. He awaited her joyful reaction. Would she need a napkin to wipe away happy tears?

"Jack, what is this?" Her voice was deadpan. Her expression looked like she was addressing a jury.

"Can't you tell?"

"I know that this is an engagement ring. What are you trying to say with it?"

"That I want to marry you."

She closed the box and laid it on the table exactly half way between them. "Jack, I thought we had an understanding. We said we didn't want to get married, didn't we?"

She had a point. When he moved back to Jackson, the city he grew up in, they became reacquainted and discovered each other all over again. They had dated in high school, but a year after graduation he was gone. There was a tour of duty in the military, a brief, failed marriage, and then a twenty-year career with the St. Louis Police Department, mostly as a homicide detective. After being found not guilty of killing a thug who had killed his partner, his partner's wife and their small child, Boulder had enough of working as a public servant. He returned home, hung out his shingle and began doing private detective work. One day he ran into Laura at the courthouse. That afternoon they met after work, had a drink, then dinner and a blissful conversation that lasted until after midnight. She too had a brief marriage that did not work out, but her career had blossomed. She was one of Jackson's best-known business lawyers and had become a litigator to be reckoned with. After only a few weeks they had become best friends, best couple and mutual admirers. They had enough in common to be intellectually interested in each other, but enough differences to make it interesting. It was a relationship they both cherished. It had all the benefits of marriage without any of the things that can drag it down. She lived in a house in fashionable Belhaven, a close-in neighborhood that had a house featured in Southern Living magazine about four times a year. He lived in a downtown condo overlooking Smith Park. She drove a British racing green Jaguar XJS. He drove a fully restored 1968 Camaro. She dressed in business suits and worked at a professional office. He wore chinos and Polo shirts and worked out of his home. What else could two middle-aged adults ask for in a world where marital commitment was becoming passé?

Lately he had gotten the feeling that things were beginning to change. One of Laura's friends told him that Laura really loved him. "You know she wants to spend the rest of her life with you." He looked for signs and he found them. Laura seemed to hold their kisses a little longer. They ate in each other's homes rather than out at restaurants. She talked about wanting a dog. They went to the Mississippi Animal Rescue League and brought home a happy little cocker spaniel. She named it Andy—after him. These and other signs, and his own feelings, made him feel that he'd better ask her soon. Her friend also said, "No matter what any woman says, she wants to get married."

Boulder took all of that in. He rationalized marriage. Yes, marriage could be good. He talked himself into it, bought the ring and decided to surprise her on her birthday.

After hearing her answer, he sat there for a moment feeling like a fool. His face got warm. His throat became dry and constricted. He could focus only on his plate, which was suddenly holding a bowl filled with the soup of the day. He felt nausea rise up and envelope him. This is not what was supposed to happen.

"Yes," he said, barely getting the words out. "My mistake."

"Oh, Jack," she replied. "I'm so sorry if I misled you."

"Not a problem," he said. His head was still down. He tried to swallow. He raised his eyes and saw the ring box that lay on the table like some kind of large bullet that had misfired. He reached out his left hand and slid it down into his pocket.

She reached across the table and took his hand, rubbing her thumb softly across his knuckles. "Jack, look at me." He raised his head. "I love you. You know that."

He did know that. But he also knew that he had made a stupid fool of himself. He also knew that things would never be the same between them.

"I'm sorry, but I have to leave," he said, standing up. "I'll call you later."

"Are you all right?"

"I'm fine," he said.

He walked the short block back to his condo and went straight to his bedroom. He opened the closet and found an overnighter from a luggage set that was no longer in style. He slammed it on the bed as hard as he could. It bounced up and hit him in the face, scraping his nose and drawing a small amount of blood. He threw it against the wall and uttered the foulest curse word he could come up with. Then he packed it with two pair of slacks, three shirts, underwear and a shaving kit. From his nightstand drawer he removed his .38 caliber Chief's Special and tossed it in the bag.

He locked up the condo, went to his reserved parking spot and got in the Camaro. Her 327-cubic-inch engine came to life. He headed north on Interstate 55.

CHAPTER 2

Jack Boulder's immediate goal was to put Jackson, Mississippi behind him as fast as possible. He drove fiercely, charging up close on every vehicle that was in front of him, then swerving into the left lane to pass. Traffic was heavy from Jackson to Canton then thinned out considerably by the rural community of Vaughn, site of Casey Jones' famous train wreck.

There was no cruise control on the Camaro so he glanced down often at the speedometer. Each time he checked, it told him that he was going ten miles an hour faster than he thought he was. When the windows are down, the sun is glaring and the wind is blowing there doesn't seem to be much difference between 75 miles per hour and 85 miles per hour. He had once toyed with the idea of installing air-conditioning in the car, but rejected it as not being faithful to the restoration code of conduct, if there was such a thing. He also thought about adding a nice stereo system to replace the stock AM radio that came in the car. His only concession to today's culture was an alarm system. He did not want this car stolen and stripped. The best audio electronics company in Mississippi installed a state-of-the-art system in the Camaro. If it was hot-wired or started without a special key, the engine would shut off in thirty seconds. The keyless, remote entry device had a panic button that made the horn sound intermittently as well as cause the headlights to blink on and off rapidly at high beam. There were three sets of keys: he had one, Laura had one and the other was hidden in a magnetic box attached to the inside of the chrome back bumper. He could not stand car thieves. Why some states were changing auto theft from a felony to a misdemeanor was a mystery to him.

He only planned on driving this restored car around town. When he went out of town he always rented a car. No sense in risking a breakdown in a car that was over thirty years old. This was the first time it had been this far out of Jackson.

Somewhere between the Durant and Winona exits he found an eighteen-wheeler that was running just over eighty. He snuggled in a few car lengths behind it and concentrated on matching the big rig's speed. A sense of calming down enveloped him. He took a deep breath and exhaled slowly. What was he going to do now? For the past forty-five minutes all he had been doing was just getting away. This highway would lead him up to Memphis then on to St. Louis, a place he had spent twenty years of his life. Did he want to go back there? There were good times remembered, but there was no fire in his belly to return to the Gateway City. He thought of just following the truck in front of him and seeing where it would take him. The monotony of driving finally took over.

Two hours later he approached the outskirts of Memphis. A billboard caught his eye. It advertised the schedule of the Memphis River Kings ice hockey team. He associated ice hockey and the St. Louis Blues—good memories. The sign indicated that the hockey games were held in the DeSoto County Civic Center, which was located at the Church Road exit. A few more miles and the civic center came in view on his left. He took the exit and drove to the parking lot. Unfortunately he would not be able to attend a hockey game tonight. The electronic billboard at the civic center proclaimed, "Tonight at 7:00 Oldies on the Road Concert." He ambled up to the ticket window. Behind it was an attractive girl, who could not have been over twenty years old, wearing an orange T-shirt.

"Do you have more information about this concert?"

"It's a bunch of singers from the sixties," she said. "It's almost sold out."

"Okay. I'll take a ticket. The balcony will be fine."

She typed on a computer keyboard, then handed him a ticket through a thick, glass window.

"When are the River Kings going to be playing again?" he asked.

"Not until this fall. Their season ended in April. They made it to the playoffs this year. Wait till next year."

"What are the Explorers? I saw their name on the sign coming in."

"That's our arena football team," she said.

"Thanks."

"The doors won't open until six," she said raising her eyes over his shoulder in a gesture that conveyed the message that someone was behind him.

He walked backed to his car and got inside. It was three hours until the start of the concert. He spent the next hour cruising around, then thirty minutes killing time at a fast food restaurant. He was one of the first ones inside when the civic center doors opened. He watched as the pre-concert laser show melted into the concert itself. He had forgotten how much he enjoyed oldies music. After it was over he hung around until almost everyone had gone.

Should he continue north on Interstate 55 or head south, back to Jackson? Was he being overly sensitive? Rejection is not a pleasant thing. He decided that he really didn't want to get married anyway and that it would all work out for the best. Jack Boulder was beginning to feel better. He decided to ride around in the country for a while.

He got into the Camaro and headed east on Church Road with both windows open. The June night air felt clean, warm and fresh, just like he was starting to feel. In less than a mile he was in a rural area and saw no other traffic. He shifted up into third, mashed down on the accelerator and wound out the gear. He shifted quickly into fourth as he went over a hill that made his stomach rise. For the first time since noon he managed a smile.

The flashing blue lights came out of nowhere. Oh no. He had been caught speeding. Not to worry. He could probably talk his way out of it. The officer would ask his occupation. At least that is what his old buddies always did when he was a police officer. That way he could answer that he was a retired police officer and, therefore, a member of the brotherhood. He would get a mild lecture, offer an apology and be on his way.

He pulled over and stopped in a gravel driveway. He watched in the driver's side mirror as the police officer got out, shut the driver's door and approached, right hand resting on the pistol on the gun belt, flashlight extended in the left hand.

"May I see your driver's license, sir?" This officer was all business. This officer was also a she. And SHE could not have been over twenty-five years old. She was wide and stout. She probably weighed a hundred and sixty. The short sleeves on her uniform shirt fit tight around biceps indicating that she did a lot of weightlifting.

He handed her his license and she immediately turned and walked back to her patrol car. She got inside and he watched as she lifted the microphone to her mouth. He remained seated, tapping the steering column. A few minutes later she returned.

"Mr. Boulder, the reason I stopped you is that you were traveling over twenty miles per hour over the posted speed limit. I am issuing you a ticket for speeding."

She tore paper from an aluminum clipboard and handed him a Uniform Mississippi Summons. "You can call the court official listed on the back for either a court date or the amount of the fine if you do not wish to contest the charge."

She turned around again and he took a deep breath. This was not the way he thought it would go. Boulder put the car in first gear and pulled slowly away. She remained parked on the side of the road, completing the beloved paperwork. This was not the best day of Boulder's life. He drove on until he reached an intersection. The sign read Getwell Road. That seemed like a good omen. He needed to get well. He turned left, heading north, figuring that he could loop back to Interstate 55 at a cross street.

He drove about a mile then saw a car stopped on a side road that ran through an open field toward a large grove of trees outlined in the night sky. The headlights of the car were on, the driver's door was open and the interior light illuminated the inside of the car. As he passed by the side road he glanced again at the car and saw something on the ground in front of the car. Boulder stopped, backed up and then drove slowly toward the car, a silver Honda Civic. As he pulled alongside he saw the body lying face down in the gravel of the road shoulder. He turned off his car, activated the emergency flashers and got out. Slowly he approached the Civic, its motor quietly humming.

The victim was a male, wearing blue jeans, black tennis shoes and a blue and white jersey. A baseball cap lay on the ground a foot and a half from the head. Boulder leaned down and detected a crimson-colored, small round spot behind the left ear. The head was turned sideways, eyes and mouth wide open. No cardiopulmonary resuscitation would be needed here.

This was the classic assassination pose. Organized crime groups and gangs would sometimes kill by having the victim get down on his knees then shoot him point blank in the back of the head. The method of execution served the purpose of making certain that the victim died instantly and sent a message to others who would cross the group.

Boulder's police instinct kicked in and he froze, looking around for footprints or items on the ground. If the weapon had been an automatic pistol, a shell casing would probably be somewhere nearby. Above all, evidence should be protected at a crime scene.

Suddenly, he heard the squealing tire noise of a car turning fast off Getwell Road onto the side road where he was standing. It was a full-sized car and it was approaching fast. Boulder stepped toward the Civic. The big car screeched to a halt, yellow lights began rotating on its roof, and a spotlight lit up on the driver's side. He was blinded. A voice came through the dark night air, "Don't move or I'll blow you away."

CHAPTER 3

Slowly and carefully, Boulder raised his hands up and out to shoulder height, like at an airport search. He attempted to see who it was, but the spotlight still blinded him.

A gravelly voice beside the spotlight said, "This is unit one. Advise Southaven P. D. to respond to Snowden Grove A-S-A-P."

"Ten four unit one," said an electronically amplified voice from a speaker in the grill of the car with the spotlight. "Which part of Snowden Grove should they come to?"

"They will see my yellow lights."

Boulder moved his left hand to the front of his face to shield the light from his eyes and cocked his head slightly to see who was standing there. Beside the light he made out a pistol—a big pistol—a .357 Magnum. A large hand with hairy knuckles gripped it and it was pointed right at Boulder. Knowing that the police were on the way Boulder figured that the best thing he could do was remain in his present position. He could do his explaining to them.

Thirty seconds later the sound of sirens came from the north followed by the approach of flashing blue lights. A Southaven police cruiser turned quickly onto the side street and pulled up behind the car with the spotlight.

A uniformed officer got out. A door slammed shut.

"Whatcha got Haggard?" asked the police officer.

"Routine patrol when I came upon this."

Another police car arrived. Boulder felt like he was on display.

"Move to your right to the center of the road and get down on your knees," commanded the voice of the police officer.

Boulder did as instructed, and then laced his fingers behind his head before the police officer could ask him. Boulder knew the drill well because he had been on the other side of it many times.

Another patrol car arrived and up the main road flashing red lights of an ambulance appeared. Boulder cut his eyes toward the spotlight car. The .357 had been returned to the holster. The officer patted him down thoroughly.

"Do you have any identification on you?" asked the officer.

"In my wallet. Back left pocket."

Boulder felt a hand reach into the pocket and remove the wallet.

"What is your name?" the officer asked.

Boulder was immediately impressed with this officer. Less experienced officers would have asked if he was Andrew Jackson Boulder, the name on the driver's license. If Boulder had stolen the wallet he might not have known the name in the wallet or would have mispronounced it. Several times in his career he had asked suspects their names and they did not match the name in the wallet. Good probable cause that something needed further investigation.

"Jack Boulder."

"What are you doing here?"

"I was driving down that road out there when I saw the lights on this parked car and stopped to see if the driver needed help. You can see what I found."

"Where are you from?"

"Jackson, Mississippi," Boulder replied.

"Where were you earlier tonight?"

"At the concert at the coliseum or civic center or whatever it's called," he said.

"Do you have a ticket stub?" the officer asked.

"No. I threw it away, I think," he said.

"Alright, Mr. Boulder. It's going to be necessary for you to go to the station while we do some further investigation."

"Am I under arrest?"

There was no reply. The officer gripped Boulder's arm, stood him up and led him to the back door of the patrol car. The handcuffs were applied and he was placed in the back seat. Boulder sat upright and the door closed. He did not even think about trying to open the door. He was now caged.

Blue and red lights swiped the trees at the edge of the field. Two-way radio static zapped the air. Muffled voices permeated the car that he was locked in. With each passing moment he felt less confident of being able to explain his way to freedom. The police were not going to release a man found at the scene of a homicide. Activity increased. Yellow crime scene tape appeared. Had they forgotten about him? Boulder wanted to say, "You-hoo, over here in the police car."

They poked their heads in the Camaro, then opened both doors and shined flashlights around the interior. One officer took the keys out of the ignition and opened the trunk. He and another officer shined light into the space. One officer reached in the trunk and stayed bent over for what seemed like a couple of minutes. He reached into his shirt pocket and removed a silver writing pen. He bent back down into the trunk again then slowly rose, holding his prize in front of him. The pen was in the trigger guard of Boulder's .38 Chief's Special revolver. Boulder heard him say, "Well, look what we have here."

The driver's door on the car in which Boulder was sitting opened. The officer got inside, turned around and held up a card.

"This is to advise you that you are under arrest for murder. You have the right to remain silent. If you answer any questions you have the right to stop answering at any time. You have the right to an attorney. If you cannot afford an attorney, one will be appointed for you." The officer looked directly at his prisoner in the back seat. "Do you understand these rights that I have read to you?"

"Of course," Boulder said.

The officer turned forward and cranked the vehicle. He picked up the microphone on the dash and said, "Unit three thirteen enroute to station with prisoner in custody. Show Miranda read."

"Ten-four, three thirteen," replied a voice from a speaker under the dashboard.

"Do you want to hear my side of the story?" Boulder asked.

"Let's wait a few minutes. You can tell your side of the story at the police department," the officer replied.

It was a short ride to the Southaven Police Department, a modern, one-story brick building on Northwest Drive, near Interstate 55 and Stateline Road. Boulder was taken inside and placed in a small interview room. The thought of being there for long did not bother him. The police would soon conclude that he had nothing to do with this homicide.

At the crime scene, activity increased rapidly and dramatically. A murder in Southaven, Mississippi is an unusual occurrence. Yellow crime scene tape ringed the immediate area. The medical examiner and the chief of detectives were called to the scene. Lights lit up the darkness as a search was made of the ground around the immediate area.

Forty-five minutes later a middle-aged detective in

khakis and a black polo shirt with the Southaven Police logo on it, entered the room. He had a thick, dark mustache, a full head of hair and a belt that carried a badge, a nine-millimeter pistol and a set of handcuffs.

"I'm Lieutenant Moulder," the officer said.

"Are you really charging me with a crime?" Boulder asked.

"Affirmative."

"When do I get to make my telephone call?"

"You can make it right now." A telephone was brought into the room and the line inserted into a wall connection.

Boulder debated whether to call his corporate attorney girlfriend Laura or Jim Darlington, a criminal defense attorney in Jackson for whom he had worked several cases. If he called Laura she might think that this was somehow connected to today's lunch fiasco. He did not need or want any sympathy from her at this point so he dialed the number of the defense attorney. A recording informed him that if the call was an emergency he could page the attorney at another number. He dialed it and then heard another recording; he did not like what it said. "This is the voicemail of Jim Darlington. I'll be out of the office on vacation until July the fifth. If your call is an emergency, please call the law firm of Bowden and Powell at..."

Boulder hung up without listening to the number. He did not relish the idea of starting over with some new law firm. Jim Darlington was one of the toughest criminal lawyers in Mississippi. Boulder wanted him. He considered calling a contact at the Department of Public Safety in Jackson, but doing so would reveal that he had been arrested. He rejected that idea. He thought of a few more names, but none of them inspired him. Besides, it was almost midnight. He picked up the telephone and punched in Laura's home number.

"You've reached the voicemail of Laura Webster. Please leave a message and I will call you back."

"Laura, this is Jack. If you are there please pick up the telephone. I need ..."

There was a click and then her voice. "It's me, Jack. Where have you been? I've been calling you all night."

"I'm at the police department in Southaven, Mississippi," he said.

"Oh my gosh. What for?"

"I believe they said suspicion of murder."

"There is no such thing as suspicion of murder in Mississippi. I'm on the way," she said firmly and urgently.

"Wait a minute," he said. "It's midnight and if they charge me with murder they won't set bail—that is, if they set bail—until tomorrow. It's the middle of the night and there is nothing you can do until tomorrow. I'll be fine. A night in jail never hurt anybody."

"Like I said, I'm on the way," she said. "Speaking as your lawyer, do not under any circumstances answer any

27

questions. If they want to interview you, tell them you would like to help, but your lawyer has advised you not to say anything. That is very important, Jack."

"I understand," he said.

"I don't think you do. You have always been on the other side of the fence. You will want to help them. I repeat: Do not answer any questions."

"Yes, ma'am."

"One more thing," she said.

"What's that?" asked Boulder.

"Where are you?"

Boulder looked at Lieutenant Moulder and asked where he was. "You are at the Southaven Police Department, but by the time she gets here you will be at the county jail in Hernando." He conveyed the information to her.

"There is still one more thing," she said.

"And that is?" Boulder asked.

"I love you."

"I love you, too."

CHAPTER 4

The Southaven detective handed the telephone to a uniformed officer who took it and left the room.

"Tell me about yourself," Lieutenant Moulder said.

"Anything specific?" Boulder asked. "I already told you where I was tonight. You have my address in Jackson."

"How long have you been a private investigator?"

"Since I moved back to Mississippi five or six years ago."

"Where did you live before then?" Lieutenant Moulder asked.

"St. Louis," Boulder said. "I was on the police department there for twenty years."

That was all it took. The two talked police work, Boulder totally disregarding his attorney's advice. The conversation switched back and forth between law enforcement and private detective work. Boulder was supplied with plenty of coffee and after forty-five minutes Lieutenant Moulder left to check on something. Boulder knew that they were processing the crime scene and doing the preliminary investigation even though it was the middle of the night. Besides, he had no place else to go.

Lieutenant Moulder returned shortly and informed Boulder that he was now being transferred to the county jail in Hernando, which was the county seat and was a few miles down Highway 51. Boulder was transported there in a marked patrol car, booked and placed in a cell by himself. Eventually he drifted off to sleep.

Just after dawn Boulder was awakened by the noise and banter of shift change. He sat up and surveyed his surroundings. It had not been a bad dream. He had been arrested. Wait a minute. Laura said she was on her way. That was around midnight. It takes no more than three and a half hours to drive from Jackson. Boulder called for the jailer and asked if there had been any contact from his attorney. "She left Jackson about midnight and should have been here long ago," Boulder explained.

The jailer said he would check on it. Ten minutes later he returned.

"What kind of car does she drive?" he asked.

"A green Jaguar," he answered.

"The State Police are working an accident on the interstate near Grenada. They have a Jag over the embankment. It caught on fire, but they can't find the driver."

Boulder grabbed the cell bars with both hands. He started moving back and forth like a caged animal. "Look, I've got to get out of here," Boulder told the jailer. "What time is it?"

The jailer looked down at his wristwatch and said, "6:50."

"What's my bail? I have to go find her."

"Right now there is no bail," he said.

"When is my bail hearing?"

"That's all I know, so that's all I can tell you."

"How about the telephone?" Boulder asked. "Can I make a couple of calls?

"Bail I can't do a thing about," he said. "A telephone I can handle." He took Boulder to a holding room with a telephone. "It has to be either local or an eight-hundred number. If you need a bail bond person, let me know."

Boulder dialed in the code for his long distance company and called Laura's cell phone number. If she was in the woods or pinned under something or whatever, then maybe she could answer it. If she had a cell phone, though, she would have used it to call out. But maybe she was trapped and couldn't call. He wasn't thinking coherently. A voice in the cell phone said that the customer he had reached was not available. He almost yelled, "Then where is she?"

Next he dialed her home number. Again he got a recording, but her voicemail was on it. He did not leave a message. What was he going to do now? The deputy did not seem to mind his using the telephone. It appeared that they understood his dilemma.

Boulder couldn't think of anyone else to call at 7:00 in the morning. The jailer took him back to his cell. He caught himself thinking a prayer. Not saying a prayer, but thinking a prayer. He would spend the rest of his life in jail if Laura's life could be spared. He was beginning to imagine the worst. Once, when he was a patrol officer he worked an accident where a truck caught on fire and burned to a black crisp in the shape of its frame. A witness reported seeing someone running from the burning truck. The officers assumed it was the driver. It wasn't until the truck had been towed in that the body of the driver was found behind the seat. His body was not even recognizable as a body. It was like black charcoal. The thought of Laura being burned alive made him nauseous. He thought he was going to throw up. Yes, Lord, he would make that deal. Let her be spared. "My life in jail for her," he thought to himself.

The jailer returned and said, "There's a telephone call for you. You can take it in the room."

Please let it be Laura.

"Hello," he said. Usually he answered with his name.

"Mr. Boulder?" It was a husky male voice.

"This is Trooper Calvin with the state police. A Ms. Laura Webster asked that I call and tell you that she is in the Grenada Hospital, and that you will be contacted by a lawyer at eight this morning."

"How is she? What happened?"

"It appears that a deer ran out in front of her car last night on the interstate just south of the Grenada county line. She has a broken arm and some bruises. The doctor wants her to stay in hospital for observation until further notice. She is a very lucky woman."

"Last night they said the car caught fire," he said.

"Yes sir," he replied. "She got out of the car before it caught fire. She passed out in the woods and it took a few minutes to find her."

"Thank you very much, Trooper," he said. And thank YOU very much, Lord, he added internally.

Suddenly, his problem seemed so small.

CHAPTER 5

The lawyer arrived at 8:30 a.m. He was an old man pushing seventy years of age. Even though it was a Mississippi June, he wore a three-piece navy blue suit with a white shirt and dark necktie. His face was ruddy and red; his hair was snow white. His teeth were yellow. He was just over six feet tall. His chest concaved in; his belly pooched out. His eyes were set in sockets under thick white eyebrows. He and Boulder were escorted to an interview room.

"Laura Webster called me," he said in a strong, throaty bass voice. "Said you and she were good friends and that you needed a lawyer in a bad way."

"That would be correct," Boulder said.

"Tell me about it."

Boulder told him about the previous evening, beginning with the traffic stop.

"Where were you before that?" he asked.

Boulder told him about the concert.

"Why were you in Southaven?"

He told the old attorney about the whole day, amending it to say that he and Laura had lunch together and not going into the details of their conversation.

"Laura's a sweet girl," he said. "And a heck of a lawyer."

"What's the process here?" Boulder asked.

"You are entitled to bail, and I expect it to be high. I called the municipal judge in Southaven and he has agreed to have a bail hearing at 10:00 tomorrow morning. I will speak to the district attorney and the detective assigned to this case. You will have to spend at least one more night here. Unless something changes I will see you tomorrow morning at the same time." He stood up slowly. "I told the police that you want to cooperate in every way possible and that I would make you available on a moment's notice. The Southaven police department is already conducting an intense investigation."

"I understand," Boulder said. "By the way, how long have you known Laura?"

"A long time," he said. "She helped me win one of the biggest cases of my career when she was in law school. I'm on my way to Grenada to see her now."

"Tell her that I'm thinking about her."

"I will."

"Oh," said Boulder. "What's your name?"

"Stallman. Jefferson Stallman."

CHAPTER 6

Boulder spent Thursday and Thursday night in the DeSoto county jail. At 7:30 a.m. on Friday morning the jailer came in and delivered homemade biscuits with gravy, two sausage patties, coffee and a newspaper.

The jailer was a frail man in his late sixties, with gray hair and blue eyes that moved from side to side when he talked. He stooped forward slightly when he walked and could not have weighed over one hundred-fifty pounds. He wore a freshly starched deputy uniform and a large black belt from which hung a large ring of jail door keys. Boulder wondered why such a man would be given jailer responsibilities until he saw the video camera above the door to the cellblock. Boulder envisioned a burly linebacker of a deputy with a big nightstick and a slapjack in his back pocket sitting at a desk outside the door watching a monitor.

"Are you somebody famous?" the jailer asked.

"Who me?" Boulder answered.

"Yeah."

"Not that I know of. Why?"

"Jeff Stallman doesn't just represent anybody these days. He handles only the rich and famous. If you're not famous, then you must be rich."

"I'm not rich or famous," Boulder said. "I'm just a man who was in the wrong place at the wrong time."

"Mrs. Vickers made these biscuits," the old jailer said. "They're the best biscuits in DeSoto county. People get arrested just so they can spend the night in jail and have some of Mrs. Vickers biscuits."

"I'll keep that in mind," Boulder said, taking the tray through the slot in the cell door.

He spread the newspaper on the cot and took a sip of coffee. The headline of the *DeSoto Times Today* blared, "Youth Baseball Coach Murdered." The article gave the details.

Late Wednesday evening Southaven police responded to Snowden Grove Park where the body of Randall Crowley, a local youth baseball coach, was discovered. He had been shot once in the head. A private investigator, Andrew Jackson Boulder, of Jackson was taken into custody and is being held for the murder.

According to Southaven P. D. Captain George King the department received a call from a security guard company at approximately 10:45 p.m. requesting assistance at the park. When police arrived they found Crowley face down in front of his car and the private detective from Jackson in the custody of the security guard.

"I was on routine patrol in the area when I heard a gunshot and checked it out," said Harold Haggard, owner of Bull's-Eye Security Services of

Southaven. "I discovered a man standing over another man, who was face down on the ground. It was obvious that the victim was deceased so I immediately secured the scene and contacted the police department."

The victim was identified as 29-year-old Randall Crowley, an employee of SVN Technology Services of Mississippi. He was also coach of the Brown Properties youth baseball team.

"We had played a game earlier in the evening," said Al Basenburger, the team's assistant coach. "We finished at nine o'clock. I guess Coach Crowley left something behind in the dugout and went back to get it. I still can't believe it. He was a good coach and a good man. We are concerned now about how to handle it with our players and their families." Basenburger said that there was a team meeting scheduled for later this afternoon and a trained grief counselor from Baptist Memorial Hospital DeSoto would be at the meeting to offer assistance. The team's Monday night game has been cancelled.

Ed McGreely, President of SVN Technology Services, said that Crowley was a computer programmer and an ideal employee. "He was conscientious and reliable. He did not miss one day of work last year. He was very well-respected by *management and fellow employees."*

Rachael Crowley Adkins, the victim's sister, said that Randall Crowley had lived in Southaven all his life. "He graduated from Southaven High and then went to Northwest Community College. He got a computer programming degree. He loved computers. I hope whoever did this gets the death penalty. My brother never hurt anybody."

Police are disclosing few details about the suspect; however, this newspaper has learned that he is a private detective in Jackson, Mississippi. Jefferson Stallman, a local attorney known for his criminal defense work in Mississippi and Tennessee, is representing him. Stallman said that he would ask for a reasonable bond, saying that Boulder is not a flight risk. "Mr. Boulder is a respected member of the community in Jackson and is willing to assist the local police in every way to solve this case."

A hearing has been set for Friday morning in Municipal Court."

Boulder read the last line again. At least there was about to be some movement on his case.

Just as he had promised, Jefferson Stallman arrived at 8:30 a.m. The old lawyer conferred with someone in another part of the building then accompanied the jailer to Boulder's cell. The jailer opened the cell door and said, "You're free to go."

The words were music to Boulder's ears, but flat music nonetheless. He wanted to know more. When they got outside he probed Stallman.

"Why aren't they going to charge me?" he asked.

"They charged you," Stallman replied. "You are out on bail. A court date will be set soon."

"What?" Boulder asked. "I thought there would be a bail hearing."

"We had it already."

"What was bail set at?"

"Five hundred thousand dollars," Stallman replied as they walked across the lawn toward the street.

"But who put up my bail? I don't know anybody around here with that kind of money."

"They take property bonds as well as cash."

"Like I said, who put up my bail?"

Stallman stopped and pointed to a white Lincoln Continental. "The lady sitting in that car."

CHAPTER 7

The power window whirred down and there on the front seat was a tired-looking, black-eyed Laura Webster. She managed a painful smile and put her hand on the door. Boulder grabbed it with both hands and reached in and kissed her on the cheek.

"Careful, Tiger," said Stallman. "She's pretty bruised up. Hop in. We'll go to my office and talk."

As they drove to Stallman's office, Laura told them about her accident. She was driving north on Interstate 55 when a huge deer ran across the highway directly into the front of her car. It bounced on the hood, then the front window and then the roof. Laura went off the side of the road and down an embankment. The state trooper estimated that her Jag rolled over at least four times. According to the state police, she had managed to unbuckle her seat belt and get away from the car before it caught on fire. She blacked out and was found in a small gully that kept her hidden from searchers for almost two hours. The next thing she remembered was waking up in the hospital.

They arrived at the law office of Jefferson Stallman, Esquire. It was located on Highway 51 just south of Stateline Road/Main Street in a single story strip mall. The outside looked like other buildings in the area, but it belied what was inside the office of the senior attorney. The reception room was filled with photographs of Stallman and famous people. On one wall there was Stallman and governors and members of Congress, on another there was Stallman and famous people from the entertainment world and on another was Stallman fishing the saltwater of the Caribbean.

"Laura, I knew that you knew some people who were well-connected, but judging by the photographs, this gentleman has some horsepower."

"Not only that," she said. "He has represented all of them legally in one manner or another."

"I feel a little better about my case now," he said. "Not that I was worried before."

"Mind if we sit down," said Laura. "I'm feeling a little woozy from the pain pills."

They proceeded to the conference room and sat down at a large mahogany table. In this room the walls were decked with paintings of landscapes. They appeared genuine and expensive.

"Mind if I get some information about Southaven before we begin?" Boulder asked.

Stallman was quick to respond. "In Southaven people are proudest of their rapidly developing economy. The old-timers, those who grew up in DeSoto county, are no longer the majority. On any given working day, a dozen new residents will make Southaven their home. Unlike some towns in America that eye new residents suspiciously, Southaven, Mississippi, has gotten good at welcoming newcomers. It's a good thing too because new residents are moving in by the drove. In 2000, DeSoto County, Mississippi, was one of the fastest-growing counties in the United States. Of course, growth is a two-edged sword. All those rooftops provide a tempting supply of property taxes for supervisors and city officials and school boards to appropriate, but building new roads and schools and water/sewer systems is an expensive proposition.

"Southaven came to grips with the growth and decided that even though the look of sprawl may have gotten a toehold it was not going to get a foothold. The City Fathers and others decided that even though there was no such thing as the old, historic downtown Southaven there could be a planned area that would be the next best thing. The 51 Main Street organization was formed in 2000 and Stateline Road was changed to Main Street.

"If you're looking for famous people from Southaven we have three of them. John Grisham had a law office here and represented this area in the Mississippi Legislature before he became a household name. And Jerry Lee Lewis lives not very far down the road. And then there's Elvis. Although he's not technically from Southaven, he owned a ranch right outside of town. His footprints are all over this area. There's probably not a person over fifty years of age in Southaven who doesn't have an Elvis Presley story. Elvis' home, Graceland, is just up the Highway 51. A few blocks up, Main Street turns into Elvis Presley Boulevard.

"What else do you want to know about Southaven?"

"That's enough information to process for now," Boulder said.

Stallman leaned forward and said, "Let's get to work. From what I can tell, the police don't really believe you had anything to do with the murder, but they don't have any other suspects. There is an assistant district attorney who is saying that you're the type of guy who could be a hit man of some kind, that you might have been hired to do a job."

"That's ridiculous."

"Of course it is," the attorney said. "But that's one of the rabbits that the hound dogs are chasing right now. The police will probably want to interview you again," he said. "I told them they could not do so without me being present. You have nothing to say that could conclusively clear you, so there is no use giving them material to hang you with."

"I'll remember that," Boulder said.

"Let's review our situation," said Stallman. "The only thing the police have on you is that you were found at the scene. You had a gun, but it does not match what appears to be the murder weapon. You did not know the victim, nor did you have a motive for killing him. Any reasonable person on a jury would vote to find you innocent of murder. On the other hand, these are not reasonable times and I am finding less and less confidence in juries' abilities these days. The police charged you, as they should have, but I have it on good authority that Lieutenant Moulder feels that you did not commit the crime. Therefore, it is my opinion that the best thing to do, while this case is fresh, would be to hire a private investigator to see what we can come up with."

"Are you kidding? I'm a private investigator."

"The lawyer who represents himself has a fool for a client," Stallman said. "I hope that's not true for detectives."

"Not in this case," Boulder said.

"Then put your private detective skills to work and find out who might have wanted Randall Crowley dead."

"Do you know anything about the victim?" Laura asked Stallman.

"No," said Stallman. "But I'm having someone check further on SVN Tech, which was his employer. Looks like they might be overextended at the bank. We should have more information early next week." Stallman picked up a pen and put it to his chin. "But one thing keeps nagging at me."

"What's that?" Boulder asked.

"The newspaper said that the first person on the scene was from Bull's-Eye Security," said Stallman. "The police told me that it was Harold Haggard himself. He is someone I would not trust at all."

"Why?" he asked.

"He retired from the Army about six years ago," said

Stallman. "He grew up in rural DeSoto county, out from Hernando, then left and went away for a long, long time. He came back and twice ran for sheriff a few years ago. Those political races were really, really messy. He spread dirt like a Delta farmer spreads fertilizer. He circulated photos of the incumbent sheriff with a woman in the back seat of a patrol car. It turned out that they were computer enhanced, but it almost cost the sheriff his job. He shows up at all kinds of police calls. He's got a scanner with him all the time. His security guard company gets a lot of jobs in Memphis, but not many businesses here in Southaven will hire him. Word is that he has made a few threats here and there."

"Do you think he has something to do with this?" Laura asked.

"I have no reason to," Stallman said. "But anytime Harold Haggard is around, things start smelling bad. He's a bully. No, I would go further than that. He's a dangerous man."

They talked some more about the case and about Boulder's current clients. Stallman informed Boulder that his car had been towed and that he could get it back today. The police were going to release Boulder's pistol as well. Laura grew more tired. Her case in Jackson had been continued due to her accident, but she needed to return to the capitol city.

"One more thing," said Stallman. "If you are going to find this killer, you need a place to stay in

Southaven." He handed Boulder an envelope with a set of keys. "These fit a little rental house I own right off Stateline Road. You can stay there."

Stallman drove Boulder to the garage where the Camaro had been impounded. Boulder then went to Southaven Pontiac Buick GMC and rented a Buick LeSabre for the drive back to Jackson, knowing that Laura would not be comfortable riding in the Camaro with no air-conditioning. They would relax over the weekend and he would return to Southaven on Monday morning. He stopped by a shop named Clothes Encounters and bought her a silk scarf to use as a sling for her arm, then went back to Stallman's office and picked up Laura. She slept soundly all the way back to Jackson.

Their weekend went exactly as planned, which is to say that they had no plan. Boulder picked up prescription painkillers, soup and ice cream while Laura rested. They never discussed their relationship or the birthday lunch last Wednesday at the University Club. They were simply content to be with each other.

On Sunday night Boulder received a call from Jefferson Stallman's assistant, Janine Beamer.

"You are coming back to Southaven, aren't you?" she asked seriously.

"Yes," he said. "First thing tomorrow morning. Why? What has happened?"

"Mr. Stallman had a heart attack last night. He's in the hospital."

CHAPTER 8

On Monday morning Boulder headed back up to Southaven. He returned the rented Buick and picked up the Camaro. He drove to Baptist Memorial Hospital DeSoto and learned that Stallman would have heart surgery later in the morning and be there for a week before being released. Miss Beamer, Stallman's long-time assistant, had been maintaining a vigil at the hospital. She told Boulder that one of Stallman's associates would take over his legal representation, and she would give him a name later. Boulder went to the hospital's front desk and got directions to the chamber of commerce. He needed a local map and as much information as he could gather about the area.

He left the hospital and drove up to Stateline Road, then headed west. He was to turn left on Northwest Drive. He passed by a collection of chain motels, convenience stores with self-serve gasoline pumps, big box retailers, fast food restaurants and strip shopping centers that sprouted around just about every interstate exit in suburban America. As he passed under the massive concrete bridge of Interstate 55 he saw blue lights flashing in his rearview mirror. What now?

He pulled over into the first driveway. It led into a small parking lot that served an old graveyard. The sign on the wrought iron fence read, "Edmundson

Cemetery." If this was an omen, it got Boulder's attention.

Once again he watched in the side mirror as a Southaven police officer approached his car. He squinted his eyes in disbelief. Not again. It looked like the same one who had stopped him before, even though all police officers can look alike when they are in uniform and have their hats on. Boulder dug for his driver's license. He had it ready for inspection as the officer arrived.

"Mr. Boulder?"

"Yes," he replied and turned toward her, the same officer who had given him the speeding ticket last week. Her muscles looked even bigger in the daylight. This time she did not have the ticket book with her.

"My name is Officer Pat Worthmore. I gave you the speeding ticket the other night."

"I know," he said cautiously.

"You don't know much about DeSoto county, do you?"

"I can't say that I do. The first time I set foot on it was the other night."

"I think I should tell you a few things about our area," she said.

"Whatever you say."

"Meet me at Snowden Grove Park at 4:00."

"Where is that?"

"Near Getwell Road and Goodman Road. That's

where you were arrested. You won't have trouble finding it."

"The Snowden Grove welcoming committee already gave me its opening reception," he said. "Why don't you just tell me right here?"

"You need help, Mr. Boulder. And I can help you. If you will be so kind as to just park in any one of the parking lots. I'll find you."

He wasn't sure what she meant, but he was in no position to refuse what might be help from a local person. She turned to walk away and he said, "Could you tell me where the chamber of commerce might be located?"

She pointed toward the west and said, "That's Northwest Drive right there at the traffic signal. Just follow it to a four-story white building. You will drive by the police department on your right."

"Thanks."

She drove away and he proceeded to the big, white building that housed the chamber of commerce. The building was also the Southaven City Hall. He went inside and found the chamber on the first floor. An attractive receptionist greeted him.

"Do you have any street maps of Southaven?" Boulder asked.

"We sure do," she replied and handed him a folded map.

He thanked her and said, "This is an interesting type of building for a City Hall. It doesn't look very government, if you know what I mean?"

"I do. And you're not the first person to comment on that." She stopped, pointed through the glass door to the hallway and said, "Wait a minute, there's John Beechnut. He's a local real estate developer. He can tell you all about this building." She waved Beechnut inside. "This gentleman was asking about the history of this building," she said as she pointed to Boulder.

"This building does have an interesting background," Beechnut said. "It was built in the mid-sixties by Allied Investment Company, which included Carey Whitehead, Kemmons Wilson and Wallace Johnson. You have probably heard of Kemmons Wilson, the founder of Holiday Inns." Boulder nodded. "You probably haven't heard of Carey Whitehead?"

"Can't say that I have," Boulder said.

"Allied Investment occupied the second and fourth floors. The fourth floor had a waterfall feature made out of Ozark Rock located on the west wall. The water was trickling all of the time. Offices were located around the elevator along the outside wall of the building and secretarial offices were outside each executive office. The building was unique, well planned and well constructed. It's made of concrete and steel. Corporate offices were upstairs, where President Carey Whitehead occupied the office on the southeast corner of the building.

"Allied Investment Company developed Southaven. They did all of the building west of Highway 51. Back

51

then, this area was home to a lot of farms, especially dairy farms. Look around at the old silos scattered around this county while you can. They will be gone soon. In 1962 they built a display of model homes on the corner of 51 and Stateline Roads and sold three hundred homes the first day.

"Allied Investment Company went public and began building Holiday Inns in the Northeast. Allied Mortgage and Development Company was opened. Allied Investment continued to loan to builders and Holiday Inns and began losing money during an economic downturn. Cary Whitehead left the company and Alidex was formed and began building inner-city housing in Chicago. Allied eventually closed.

"The building was vacant until it was purchased by Northwest Mississippi Community College. When the college moved to the newly constructed DeSoto Center on Church Road, this building was once again vacant. The City of Southaven bought the building from Jim Saucier in the late nineties and moved their offices from the corner of Highway 51 and Mississippi Valley Boulevard. Mr. Saucier donated the lake adjoining the building, and a park was created in his name—Saucier Park.

"The City of Southaven occupied the annex on the east side of the building and tenants occupied the first floor of the original building. The City has renovated the second, third and fourth floors. Tenants occupy the second and third floors. City administrative offices are on the fourth floor. The first floor houses public services like Building Permits, Planning, the City Clerk, and the Water Department. And of course the chamber of commerce is here on the first floor."

"I see," Boulder said.

"I'm sorry," Beechnut said. "You asked me what time it was and I told you how to build a watch. It's just that we're sort of proud of our little community."

"That's very impressive."

Beechnut grinned and shook hands with Boulder, then said, "Hope you have a nice time while you're here." He waved at the receptionist and walked out the door.

"Thanks. I will."

Boulder left and drove back down Northwest Drive toward Stateline/Main Street. He still had a few hours before he was to meet with Officer Worthmore. He spotted the M. R. Davis Library on his left and decided that he would stop in and do some research. Once inside, he was directed to a computer that had Internet access. He went to one of the widely-used search engines and typed in "Southaven." The first reference was to the chamber of commerce that he had just visited. Then there was one for the City of Southaven. He opened the City government site and found that:

- From 1990 to 1999, Southaven's population grew by 29.4%.

- The nation's largest Sam's Wholesale Club is located in Southaven.
- The $32 million DeSoto County Civic Center, located in Southaven is home to professional ice hockey, arena football, and more.
- Snowden Grove Park, the nation's largest youth and adult baseball complex opened in 2000.

He then surfed around the Southaven Chamber of Commerce website and found the following:

Just minutes from Memphis, Southaven is the gateway to the Mississippi Delta. Our music and literary traditions gained the state worldwide fame. Author John Grisham had a law practice in Southaven, blues grew out of the Delta, and Graceland, the home of Elvis Presley, is located just minutes away. It's less than a half-hour drive to the casinos in Tunica County, Mississippi. Blackjack, roulette, slots—they've got it all. You can also enjoy delicious dining and great shows including the likes of Jay Leno, Johnny Cash and Ray Charles.

With easy highway access, close proximity to the Memphis International Airport, emergency services, higher education, a variety of housing choices and a progressive local government and Chamber of Commerce, Southaven is a desirable residential and business community.

Again, he saw a mention of Snowden Grove Park being the nation's largest youth baseball complex and host of the Dizzy Dean World Series. That is where Officer Worthmore wanted to meet him and it was on the road leading to the park where Randall Crowley met his death.

Boulder searched some more on the Internet and found the home page of SVN Technologies of Mississippi. It seemed to be in the business of e-commerce, website design and various aspects of computer consulting. To Boulder, much of the information might have well have been in Greek. He knew more than the average person about computers and how to use them for research, but he knew little about hardware and operating software.

He entered Ed McGreely's name in a search engine and found a personal profile article in a computer magazine's website. It was titled, "Motivation and McGreely Both Begin With M—a CEO driven to succeed." According to the article, Ed McGreely was the president and founder of SVN. On his fortieth birthday he stole a weekend to take stock of his life. He rented a room at Bonne Terre, an upscale retreat in DeSoto county, and engaged himself in his own personal strategic planning retreat. In his luxurious room at the bed and breakfast facility, he posted sticky notes on the wall and listed his personal strengths and weaknesses. He envisioned the future and compared it to where he was now.

He was not satisfied with what he saw. By most measures, he was a success. He was the regional sales manager for a large telecommunications company, which had its southeastern regional office in Memphis. His job was to motivate managers of sales reps to go out and sign up new accounts. He had always thrown everything into his work.

It had cost him a marriage, but he didn't mind. His wife didn't understand business and he didn't understand her. There were two children, a twelve-year-old girl and a fifteen-year-old boy. The boy had already totaled two Jeep Wranglers, and the girl fought every night with her mother. He hated going home. Work was his life. One day he was served with divorce papers at his office. He never went back home. That very day he went to the finest department store in downtown Memphis, bought a new wardrobe and rented a condo in Harbor Town, the fashionable, planned community down by the Mississippi River near downtown Memphis.

At his personal retreat, he looked out and saw the future. He didn't like it. He would never be head of the company that he worked for. He would never own it. He decided then and there that he would form his own company, one that was in a growing industry and one that involved managing people like he was already doing. He knew that the Internet was beginning to boom and people were doing all kinds of things involving computers. He decided that he would build a new company from the ground up.

He left the retreat and went to work on his business plan. He recruited investors and computer geeks. He withdrew $25,000 from a hidden savings account. To save money, he leased twelve hundred square feet of space in an old shopping center on Highway 51 in Southaven. He started out with website design and Internet marketing. These activities did not require huge capital investments. With savvy Internet marketing, he and his few employees took one small fishing lure company in the Mississippi Delta from $30,000 in annual sales to over $1 million in less than nine months. One of his engineers designed an ordering system for a small manufacturer in central Mississippi that allowed the client's customers to do all their ordering over the Internet. A year later his company became an Internet Service Provider, offering Internet access to customers. He was written up in a computer magazine article, then a feature story in the *Commercial Appeal* newspaper and then a national business magazine named his company as one of its annual "Up & Comers." His business grew so fast the first five years that it was dizzying. He even added a pager repair operation to his business. By the end of the sixth year he had leased what was once an entire grocery store in the shopping center where he started the company. He had over a hundred employees in seven states. They were supervised by five district managers much in the same way that he did when he was a sales manager.

On the first Thursday of every month there was a managers' meeting at the corporate office in Southaven. On the Wednesday before, McGreely would dispatch the company's Cessna Citation Sovereign business jet on a loop to Dallas, Houston, New Orleans, Atlanta and Nashville to pick up the managers and bring them in for a day of reporting, analyzing and motivating. On Friday, the sleek jet would leave to return the managers to their territories. The jet aircraft was expensive, but it provided McGreely with the ambiance he desired to hire and retain only the highest-producing managers. It also provided him with the means to help politicians get from Point A to Point B. He gave rides only to incumbents, and he always went along. He bought thirty acres in the southern part of Southaven that was not yet developed and there built his mansion.

Boulder read the article again and decided that McGreely would be an interesting person to interview. But first he wanted to talk to the victim's family. He found the newspaper stacks and searched for Randall Crowley's obituary.

CHAPTER 9

According to the obituary, Randall Thomas Crowley, Jr. was succeeded by his father, Randall Crowley, Sr., his stepmother, Ruth Hogan-Crowley, and his sister, Rachael Crowley Adkins. Boulder checked the telephone book and found a listing for Randall Crowley, Sr. He called the number. A middle-aged, female voice answered. He asked if this was the residence of the parents of Randall Crowley, Jr. She said that it was.

"My name is Jack Boulder. I'm a private investigator. I found your son the other night. I had nothing to do with his death, but I would like to find out who might have killed him. May I come talk to you?"

The silence lasted about six seconds, but to Boulder it seemed like six minutes. He was not going to speak until she did.

"We live in Stonehedge," she said. "I'll be watching for you." She gave him directions, and he went to his car.

Boulder pulled into the Stonehedge residential development and immediately thought that Randall Crowley, Jr. did not come from a poor family if this is where the parents lived. He found the address and parked in front of a two-story, brick house that whispered upscale. He walked up a sidewalk across a landscaped yard and rang the doorbell as his head tilted upward toward the stained glass window on the second floor. A woman appeared at the door.

"I'm Ruth Hogan-Crowley," she said in a professional voice as she extended her hand. Boulder wondered why he was expecting a housewife. She was about fifty and had short, black hair. She had on stylish, black-framed glasses and wore a medium-blue suit that said she was a boss, not a secretary. She carried herself in the manner of someone in charge. Chin up; shoulders back. She stood every bit of five feet ten, but was thin as a fashion model. She showed no signs of grief over the death of a son.

"My name is Jack Boulder," he said. "May I talk with you about your son?"

"Come this way," she said, and led him back to a paneled office with a large window that overlooked a sculptured backyard flower garden. On the walls were certificates indicating her expertise and completion of various courses in the field of financial planning. Scanning the rest of the office Boulder saw no evidence of any kind of family. There were no framed photos of husband or son or daughter. There was nothing personal at all among her mementos. This was a woman who probably kept business and personal lives totally separate from each other. On one wall was a large map of the world. In the center of the office was a large, wooden executive desk in front of which were parked two captains' chairs. She motioned Boulder to one of the chairs in front of the desk as she sat down in the black leather chair behind the desk.

"What can I do for you, Mr. Boulder?"

"I'm the one who found your son's body the other night."

"Stepson," she corrected.

"My deepest sympathies," he said.

"Thank you."

"Could you tell me a little about him?"

"Why do you want to know?" she asked.

"Because I was at the scene when the police arrived. They charged me with murder even though I did not have anything to do with his death. I want to find out who killed your son—stepson—and why."

"What is it to you?"

"To make sure my name is cleared," Boulder said.

"Did you kill him?"

"No."

She got up from the chair and walked to the window. She placed an elbow in one hand, then the other hand to her chin. She turned, raised her eyebrows and looked at Boulder directly in the eyes.

"Randy's murder is killing his father. Whoever killed Randy is going to be responsible for the death of two people," she said.

"I really would like to find out who killed him," Boulder said, almost pleading.

"You know something," she said as she sat back

down. "In one sense, it doesn't matter who killed Randy. His father is almost catatonic. He just sits in his room upstairs. I talked to a psychologist about the stages of grief. Randall Crowley never got to the first one. It's as if he has been shot in the head as well."

"So you'll help me?"

"I'll do better than that, Mr. Boulder," she said. "You find out who killed Randy and why—and I emphasize WHY—and I will pay you $50,000. Call it a reward."

"I need to know as much as possible about Randy," Boulder said.

She sat back down and began talking. "Randy's father and I met when Randy was twenty-one years old. Let's see, that would have been about eight years ago. Randy was graduating from college with a degree in computer science. He worked for a while for Jones Davis and Associates here in Southaven. Two years ago, he went to work at SVN Tech. From what I could tell, he liked his job. He was really into technology and computers. He made a decent salary, but he didn't have any major assets.

"He had one hobby, and that was baseball. He went to every home game of the Memphis Redbirds. He's been to just about every major league baseball stadium in the country. He also coaches a youth baseball team. He's never been married and, as far as I know, has never had a girlfriend. He lived alone in an apartment on Church Road. I've never heard of him having any bad relations with anyone. He and his father were very close. What else can I tell you about him?"

"Any enemies? Anybody that he ever talked bad about?"

"Nobody," she replied. "Although I should point out that I didn't talk to Randy very much. I think he only liked me because I made his father happy."

"What happened to his mother?"

"She and Randall were divorced when Randy was twelve. Randall caught her with another man. He filed for divorce and she left town with the other man. She hasn't been back since. From what I can tell, Randall and Randy were like baseball buddies during Randy's teenage years. As a single father, Randall wanted to raise his son to be a good person. Instead of Randy running around with friends, he ran around with his father. They went to a lot of baseball games not only around here, but other cities as well. They saw a lot of major league games."

"Have you ever been inside his apartment?"

"No," she said. "I never have. I need to have his things moved and let the apartment manager know that he will not be there anymore." She picked up a pen and made a note on a desk calendar.

"Do you mind if I look at his apartment?" Boulder asked.

"No," she replied. "I'll get the key for you."

"Thank you," Boulder said, standing up. "If you

don't mind, would you also write a letter giving me permission to be in his apartment? I don't want to get arrested again."

"Just a moment," she said, turning around and typing on a computer keyboard. The printer hummed and in a moment she handed him the letter. They stood up and walked to the front door. She looked out at the street. "Is that your Camaro?"

"Yes."

"I had one almost just like it."

They bid farewell and Boulder left. Now he had a client. Well, not really a client, but another reason to find out why someone would kill a nice computer guy who liked coaching little kids.

CHAPTER 10

He killed the time by driving around some more. At 3:45 p.m. he headed out to the location of the rendezvous. Things sure looked different in the daylight. Snowden Grove Park was a large complex of baseball fields that rivaled anything he had ever seen. There were 17 fields in four- and five-field clusters. From what he could tell, it appeared that there were fields of varying sizes for different levels of league play. A chain link fence surrounded each field and the dugouts and press boxes had matching bronze-colored tin roofs. The area was manicured like a pro golf course. It reminded him of the grounds of a well-kept zoo. He pulled into the main parking lot in front of the large, red and white concession area located in the center of the complex. The place was deserted.

At 4:05 p.m. a new, bright blue Chevrolet Camaro Z-28 rounded the entrance road to the complex and headed toward him. It pulled alongside and stopped, only six inches from his car. It faced the opposite direction so that they were driver door to driver door. The throaty exhaust told him that there was a big V-8 under the hood. The driver's darkened window powered down and there in the driver's seat was Officer Pat Worthmore. Her hair was short but in a feminine cut. She had on aviator sunglasses. She was sitting low in the driver's seat of a car that was lower than his so he looked slightly down at her.

"I guess you are wondering why I called this meeting," she said. She looked straight ahead, not removing her sunglasses.

"You might say that."

"I did a little checking up on you, Andrew Jackson Boulder," she said confidently. "And I'm not quite sure about you." He let the comment pass without reply. She turned her head toward him. "You are a private detective and ex-cop. What are you doing in Southaven?"

"I had to go to the bathroom and this was the next exit."

"Are you working on a case here?"

"Yeah," he said. "I'm trying to find out who killed Randy Crowley. My client is myself. And so far I'm not making much headway. By the way, aren't you supposed to advise me of my Miranda rights before questioning me?"

"That only applies if I suspect you of committing a crime. I only suspect that you are being framed."

"And what makes you think that?"

"I gave you a speeding ticket at about the time the homicide took place. It seems to me that a murderer would be speeding away from the crime scene, not toward it."

"Did you tell that to your supervisor?" he asked.

"Of course," she said. "But when somebody catches you standing beside the body, it doesn't help your case." Another car drove into the complex and parked behind a dugout. A man got out, opened the trunk and lifted a bag with baseball bat handles sticking out. "We found the gun, you know?"

"So what? That gun hasn't been fired in a month."

"Your gun in your trunk is not the gun I'm talking about," she said. "We found a .25 caliber Saturday Night Special in the ditch, not fifteen feet from the body. Your prints are being checked against a partial print on that gun. The crime lab is also checking to see if the bullet matches the gun."

"Why are you telling me this?" he asked. "You could get into trouble."

She tightened her lips, looked forward again and said evenly, "Why did you kill that man in St. Louis?"

"You don't know? I thought you checked me out."

"I'm still working on it. All I know right now is that our district attorney's investigator said that he had checked with the St. Louis P. D. and found out you retired after being charged with murder."

"I retired after I was found innocent of murder," he said. "Don't you just love how law enforcement agencies always report the arrest on a rap sheet but don't follow up when someone is acquitted?"

"You didn't answer my question."

"The human scum that I shot murdered my partner,

his wife and little girl while burglarizing their house. And I would just as soon talk no more about it."

Another car drove into the lot and pulled up behind the car by the dugout. A door opened and two boys in baseball uniforms got out. They ran onto the baseball field and started throwing a ball back and forth.

"Looks like it's time for baseball to begin."

"In an hour this place will be packed," she said. "Do you have a place to stay?"

"Yes, my lawyer put me up in a rental house not very far from the police station," he said, wondering what she really meant. She could have just asked where he was staying. It was time to change the subject. "If you think I'm being framed, you must have some idea who framed me."

"I have a very good idea," she replied.

"Would you care to share it with me?"

"Who was the first person you saw when you were at the scene?" she asked.

"That would have been the security guard who drove up," he said.

"Do you find that a little strange?"

"Not particularly," he said.

"Why would a security guard be out here in this area? There are no office buildings or warehouses to patrol."

"Maybe he checked on this baseball facility," he said. "It's not uncommon for something like this to have security. I mean—look at this place. This is the Taj Mahal of youth baseball if you ask me. I've never seen a base-ball complex like this."

"Maybe so," she said.

"You're the second person who has mentioned this security guy. What's the deal with him?"

"He has a way of interfering often with the Southaven P. D.," she said. "It may be called Bull's-Eye Security, but we call it BS."

"You think he had something to do with that coach getting killed?" Boulder asked.

"Who knows?"

"Do you know anybody who could help me? Anybody I could interview? I thought about the rela-tives of the victim and his employer. Do you know if he had any friends I should talk to?"

"You might want to talk to his girlfriend," she said. "Her name is Melinda Craft. She's the assistant manag-er at the Kroger store. She's in the book."

Boulder pulled out a small notebook from his glove compartment and wrote down the name. "Anybody else?"

"Yeah," she said and started her car. "See that guy over there at the dugout? That's the victim's assistant coach. I've got to run. Don't tell anybody I told you to talk to them."

"What about . . ."

Her car pulled away rapidly. Boulder turned around and looked at the coach.

CHAPTER 11

Al Basenburger weighed two hundred-sixty pounds, a hundred of which was plastered onto his body between his armpits and his hips. His spare tire looked like a spare beanbag. His arms and legs, although normal, appeared spindly—like pipe cleaners poking out of a potato man. There was no neck to speak of. His chin just went straight down and connected with his chest. It was as if a bowling ball had been set on his shoulders. At one time he was a good baseball player. Rumor had it that he once played in the minor leagues.

Basenburger's main problem was not a physical one however. He was a pretty good baseball coach and he let everybody know it. He had been in several arguments with the commissioners of the league over the years, and he was a marked man when it came to coaching a team. Two years ago he shoved an umpire and half the parents withdrew their kids from his team. He was allowed to be an assistant coach, but there was an unwritten code that he would not be allowed to be the head coach. He tried to raise the issue at one of the league meetings last year, but he got nowhere with it. It was then that he came to terms with his lot in youth baseball life. He was mad, but he knew there was nothing in his power to change things. The only coach who would have him as his assistant was Randall Crowley.

Jack Boulder strode toward Basenburger as the assistant coach removed a duffel bag of baseball gear from the trunk of his car. The coach wore blue jeans and a vaguely familiar blue and white baseball jersey. "Hi, Coach," said Boulder. Basenburger turned around. "I thought you had canceled tonight's game in memory of your coach."

"We decided that the best thing to do was go ahead. Maybe the players will try to win one for the Gipper."

Boulder walked up to the assistant coach and said, "Can I give you a hand with this equipment?"

"Thanks, but I can manage."

"Are you going to be the new coach now?"

"Not likely," said Basenburger. "They suspended me from being a head coach two years ago when I got into an argument with an umpire. I thought for a minute you were the substitute head coach or something." They walked toward the first base dugout and Basenburger dropped the gear on the ground.

"My name is Jack Boulder."

"You an uncle or grandfather of one of the players or something?"

"No. I'm a private investigator. I'm interested in learning about Randy Crowley."

"Wait a minute," Basenburger said with a snap of his fingers. "You're the guy the police took in." His tone was one of admiration, as if he had met a celebrity.

"That's me. But I assure you I had nothing to do with

your coach's death."

A white Chevrolet Suburban driven by a mom pulled up and disgorged six little baseball players in uniform. They scampered to the infield and started throwing baseballs to each other, except for two who were squirting at each other with water pistols.

"All right, you guys," yelled Basenburger. "Pitch with each other till the rest of the team gets here. Especially you two with the water guns."

"How long did you know Randall Crowley?" Boulder asked.

"Just met him about three weeks before the season started. One of the nicest guys I ever met. This was his first season to be a head coach."

"Do you know anything about his family life or where he worked?"

"Randy was a single man. Worked for one of those computer companies. He told me what he did one time, but I didn't really understand it. He knew a lot about baseball though. He could tell you something about every player that ever played. And the kids liked him. I liked him, too. He let me coach."

Another car pulled up delivering more players. The coach and several players from the opposing team arrived.

"Do you know anybody who knew him well?"

"Not really. The only time I ever saw him was with the baseball team."

"Did he seem any different last Wednesday night?"

"Hmm. Now that you mention it, I guess he did. When he left after the game was over I told him that I would see him later. He said that he hoped so. I thought that was kind of a strange thing for him to say."

"Do you remember what time he left?"

The assistant coach put hand to chin and said, "Would have had to have been about 9:15. We played the 7:30 game, so it would have been over no later than 9:00. We had a short team meeting and he gave out the game ball. He always did that. Went around and mentioned every kid's name and some good thing they did that night. Then he would give one of them the game ball."

"Sounds like a nice guy."

"Yeah. I have the tendency to kick their little butts and tell them they better shape up or else warm the bench next time. But not Randy. I'm an old guy; he's a modern guy. Know what I mean?"

"I think so. Thanks. And good luck tonight."

CHAPTER 12

Boulder decided to go back to Baptist Memorial Hospital DeSoto and check on Jefferson Stallman before going to the rental house for the evening. He walked down the hall and spotted Jefferson Stallman's assistant in the reception area outside the coronary care unity. She could not have been much younger than Stallman, which is to say that she was probably in her mid- to late-sixties. She looked tired, but still businesslike with a zippered folio in one hand. She was now managing the attorney's family and friends who were coming to the hospital.

"How is he?" Boulder asked.

"The doctor says that he looks as good as can be expected. The surgery went fine. He's going to have to change his lifestyle though. All of his criminal cases are being handled by Will Zachary, one of his associates." She unzipped the folio and pulled out a card. "Here's how you can reach him."

"Thanks."

"And you can stay in the rental house as long as you like."

"Thanks," Boulder repeated. "Can I ask you something?"

"Yes. Of course."

"How did Mr. Stallman and Laura meet each other?

Did they have a case in the past?"

"Well, yes and no," Miss Beamer said. "Jefferson—rather Mr. Stallman—gives a lecture each year to the criminal law class at Ole Miss Law School. When he lectured during Laura's year they got into a big discussion on some major point of law. Mr. Stallman was very impressed with her. Just between me and you I think she was the first student to ever win an argument with him in that class. He liked her immediately. During her first year out of law school he associated her to work with him on an important case involving a large business that had been accused of bribing a public official in Jackson. She handled the research, and he handled the courtroom. The client won. Since then he has associated her on just about every case that has anything to do with criminal conduct by a business. She's one of the best corporate attorneys in the state, you know?"

"That's what I am told," Boulder said.

"Good luck with your case, Mr. Boulder. Don't worry. Will Zachary is a fine lawyer or he would not be working with Mr. Stallman."

Boulder said goodbye and went to the rental house. It was sparsely furnished but adequate. It beat staying in a motel by a long shot. He called Laura and told her about Stallman's condition and that a new attorney would be representing him. Perhaps it was because of what Miss Beamer had told him, but Boulder sensed a concern and respect in Laura's voice when she talked about Stallman. He told her about his research at the library on SVN Tech and his interviews with Mrs. Hogan-Crowley, Officer Pat Worthmore and assistant baseball coach Basenburger. She was especially interested in SVN Tech and what he had found. He gave her the Internet website addresses.

"I'll have one of our researchers get to work on SVN Tech as well," Laura said. "Maybe we can find out some more. Also, I'll call Will Zachary and let him know what we are doing on this end."

"How much is this going to cost me?" he asked. "I might need that fifty grand from the victim's stepmother."

"Did you get that in writing?" Laura snapped back.

"No, but..."

"Just remember that she has offered you a reward," Laura said. "She has not hired you. There is no fiduciary interest here. She is not your client."

"I think I understand that," Boulder said tentatively.

"You don't have to report to her, in other words. Do you know if there was an insurance policy on the victim?"

"Not yet."

"That might be good to know," Laura said. "If the family is in financial trouble . . . well, who knows?"

"You sound like yourself again. How are you feeling?"

"Much better. I'm going to go back to work tomorrow," she answered.

"I'll call every day and let you know how it's going."

"I still love you, Jack," she said softly.

"I love you,0 too."

After they hung up he found a telephone book and looked up Melinda Craft. In spite of what Officer Worthmore had told him, he introduced himself by saying that he was one of her acquaintances. He asked if he could talk to her about Randall Crowley, Jr.

"You could come by tomorrow afternoon at 3:30," she said.

Boulder sat down at the small dining room table and planned the next day. He would interview McGreely at SVN Tech in the morning and Melinda Craft in the afternoon.

CHAPTER 13

At 9:00 a.m. on Tuesday morning Jack Boulder pulled into the large shopping center parking lot on Highway 51 and immediately spotted the SVN Tech logo on the front of the building. The fact that the structure was once a large grocery store was not disguised very well. After all, from the outside, a large box is a large box. Inside the box was quite another story altogether.

Boulder walked in through a heavy, tinted glass door to be greeted by a softly-flowing, twenty-foot indoor waterfall. On either side of the waterfall were giant color screens showing an aquarium scene. The lobby was wide and high. New age music filled the air. Boulder raised his head and took it in. An evergreen fragrance permeated his nostrils.

"Good afternoon," said a pleasant voice from an attractive woman behind a desk to Boulder's left.

"Hi. I'm here to see Ed McGreely." He handed her his business card. It contained only his name and telephone number.

"May I tell him what this is in reference to?" She knew he did not have an appointment.

"Yes," said Boulder. "I'm investigating the murder of one of his employees."

"Just a moment," the woman said, picking up a telephone receiver and dialing a number. "A Mr. Boulder is here to see Mr. McGreely. Says he is investigating a murder of one of our employees." She listened and then said to Boulder. "Go through that door and down the hall to the second door on your right."

He did as instructed and found himself in a small reception room. Another woman instructed him to wait a minute and that Mr. McGreely would be with him. Boulder scanned the walls and saw framed media articles about McGreely. He did not find the one that he saw on the Internet. He read each one and learned more about the man he was about to interview. These articles were interesting, but Boulder thought they were a bit too staged. There was too much publicity agent tint on them.

Soon McGreely came out from behind the door. He was in his mid-forties and had the look of a person who ran five miles every morning and swam laps every night. The dark brown hair might have been a toupee. He had skin tanned the shade of a person who spends time at the beach or the tanning parlor. He was of medium height and had no distinguishing features that Boulder could detect. He wore a black mock turtleneck and a stylish gray suit. The jacket was unbuttoned.

"How can I help you?"

"I was wondering if I could talk to you about Randall Crowley," Boulder said.

"As I told the woman from the newspaper, he was a very good employee."

"How long had he worked for you?"

"You would need to talk to the Personnel Department about that," said McGreely.

"Where would I find them?"

He turned sideways and mockingly asked the assistant. "Am I standing here talking to a person who is a murder suspect?" She shrugged. He turned back to Boulder. "Would you please leave?"

"I'm just trying to find out who killed your employee," Boulder said. "I thought that might interest you."

"You are right. It would interest me." He placed both hands in his pants pockets, his coat pulled back in the manner of a Wild West gunslinger about to draw. He glared at Boulder. There was ten seconds of uncomfortable silence. The woman at the desk froze in place. "Do I have to call Security to get you to leave?"

Boulder said nothing, then turned and walked out of the office. He marched past the receptionist at the front and strode purposefully across the hot asphalt parking lot to his car. As he inserted the key in the lock he saw a business card stuck in the weather-stripping around the driver's window. He pulled it out and read a message printed in blue ink from a ballpoint pen. "Meet me in the Entergy parking lot at 11:30. I'll have on a red shirt."

Boulder turned over the card and looked at the other side. It was an SVN Technologies of Mississippi business card and it read, "Randall Crowley, Website Design and Programming."

CHAPTER 14

At 11:30 a.m. Jack Boulder pulled into the electric company parking lot and switched off the ignition. No sooner than he had done so, a brown Toyota Celica pulled up and parked beside him. A young man in his twenties wearing a red T-shirt and blue jeans got out and walked inside the building. He had black, kinky hair and thick glasses. On his belt was a pager. On his feet was a pair of black sneakers. Three minutes later he walked out and passed by Boulder's car on the driver's side. As he walked by the driver's side window he said, "Follow me," without turning his head. He got back into his Toyota.

Boulder followed the car out of the parking lot and then to Dale's Restaurant on Stateline Road. Boulder wiped the perspiration from his brow and followed him inside.

"Want something to eat? This is better than those franchise places. We may have to wait a minute. Everybody comes here for lunch."

Momentarily, they were seated. Each ordered the blue plate special, Boulder delighted to find fried okra on the menu. The stranger pushed his thick glasses back up on his nose, raised his head and looked at Boulder.

"You're the one working on Randy's case, aren't you?"

"More or less. Mostly more."

"There are some things I think you should know about where he worked."

"Who are you?" Boulder asked.

"Jamie Whatley. I worked with Randy doing website design. There were five of us. Randy got shot last week and I got laid off yesterday, so now there are only three."

The server brought their lunches and they dug in. Jamie Whatley cut up his chicken fried steak, chewed a bit, pushed the glasses up and took a sip of iced tea through a straw.

"Must be tough losing your job," Boulder said. "I hear there are a lot of layoffs these days."

"Not in my business," Whatley said. "I've already got another job. Report tomorrow morning."

"So what do I need to know?"

"Something's going on at SVN Tech. They're laying off people left and right, man. All of a sudden, too. It doesn't make sense. We've got plenty of work. Talk around our office was that we are about to lose our biggest pager repair account. It's worth millions. If that was true, they would be laying off repair guys, not people in the website section. Website design is behind as it is. The website is generating more business for our company than the field people. Man, you would not believe how the field people at SVN Tech are treated compared to the inside people who do the work."

"Give me an example," Boulder said.

"Easy," Jamie Whatley replied. "The first Thursday of every month is the big day at SVN Tech. They take the company jet, pick up the district managers and bring them in for a big rah-rah meeting. You ought to see that jet. It lands over at the airport in Olive Branch on the Wednesday afternoon before First Thursday. McGreely takes the district managers out to eat on Wednesday night, then First Thursday begins.

"Everybody has to clean up the workspace for First Thursday. All the employees go into the auditorium and we do cheers—can you believe that?—cheers! It's crazy to me, man. It's like we're one of those multi-level, pyramid things or something. The website team thinks it's a big joke, but Ed McGreely thinks First Thursday is why SVN Tech is so successful. Then on Friday morning the jet takes off and takes the mighty district managers back to their districts."

"What does that have to do with your co-worker?"

"I don't know," Whatley said. "But Randy told me that if anything happened to him it wasn't an accident." He pushed up his glasses again and took another bite. "And, man, something happened to him."

"Why are you telling me?"

"I can't tell anybody at work because I just got fired. I called Randy's dad to tell him last night, but he's freaked out, man. Randy's stepmother told me to tell you."

"Did you talk personally with Randy's father?"

"No. Just his stepmother," said Whatley. "Anyway, you're supposed to be a detective, aren't you?"

"That's what they say," Boulder said. "How did you know who I was?"

"Man, everybody in town knows who you are. You were in the newspaper and you drive an old Camaro around that looks brand new. I saw your car at SVN Tech this morning. You were easy to find."

"Did anything unusual happen last Wednesday, the day that Randy was killed?"

"That's the day he told me he thought he was in trouble."

"For what?"

"On Tuesday, the day before, he was outside the president's office and heard some stuff that he shouldn't have. He said that he heard McGreely and some security guy talking about how to make it look like an accident. He said that one of them said that they would be lucky if all twelve of them went down. It scared the you-know-what out of Randy. I've never seen him like that. He was shaking, man."

"Anything else?"

"Randy thinks they saw him leave. It scared him so much he left his car in his apartment parking lot and had me pick him up at the Mississippi Valley Gas parking lot. He spent the night with me Tuesday night. We went back to his apartment at lunch on Wednesday. And guess what?"

"What?"

"Randy taped a piece of tape to the door when he left on Tuesday and it was pulled apart on Wednesday. Somebody had been in his apartment Tuesday night." Whatley let his information sink in on Boulder. "Pretty strange, huh?"

"Yes," Boulder said. "How did Randy get along with people at work?"

"Everybody liked Randy, man."

"So what do you think is going on?"

"I don't know," Whatley said. "All I know is I want to get out of there."

"How can I get in touch with you?"

Whatley fished in his jeans pocket and pulled out another of Randy Crowley's business cards. He pushed his glasses up on his nose again and wrote something on the card. "Here's my home telephone number and my pager number."

CHAPTER 15

Melinda Craft was a young, gentle-looking woman, somewhere closer to motherly than homely. Her straight, light brown hair was silky and clean. Her face was unblemished, her eyes large and her eyebrows thick, like they had never been plucked. She was average weight and average height for a woman of thirty-one, that is to say that there was nothing particularly distinctive about her physical features. But her personality was there in her eyes and in her smile. She wore a green summer dress. Everything about her was pleasant.

She and Jack Boulder were seated in the living room of her modest suburban, ranch-style home. The place was neat and clean. An air-conditioner hummed in the background. On an end-table by the sofa was an eight-by-ten photograph of a couple in their sixties. On the wall opposite the sofa hung a large framed photo of Melinda Craft and her son. It had the flavor of one of those photos that the church photographers sell to families after they have their pictures taken for the church directory.

Through the hall door Boulder could see into the son's room. There was a poster depicting a professional baseball player in the middle of a mighty swing. Soccer and baseball trophies and medals were displayed in a shelf. The bedspread was red, white and blue.

"Thank you for seeing me," he said. "I promise I didn't have anything to do with Randy's death." Boulder almost said the word "murder" but figured that "death" would be more appropriate. In all his years of death notifications he never felt that there was a right thing to say when talking about someone else being killed.

"Pat said that she didn't think you had anything to do with it," she said. "That's good enough for me."

"When was the last time you saw him?" he asked, almost adding the word "alive."

"I saw him Wednesday night at Adam's game. The last time would have been about 9:00 when the game ended."

"Did you talk to him then?" he asked.

"Only to tell him that he coached a good game," she said. "We won six to three. Adam got on base every time."

"Good," he replied.

"Randy said at the beginning of the season that what was most important was to get on base. It didn't matter if the batter got a hit or a walk or got hit with a pitch. A team could not score a run if it did not put runners on the bases. He was a good baseball coach."

"How did you two meet?"

"We met at Springfest, just a few months ago," she said. "We worked as volunteers in the same concession booth. Have you ever been to Springfest?"

"No. I'm afraid not. I've never been in Southaven

until last week."

"You must come back next year. If you like old cars, and I can see that you do, you will love it," she said as she turned her head to the front window. "There's lots of music, games and fun. The antique car parade gets bigger and better every year. It's one of the things you can't miss about Springfest."

"I see."

"The other thing is barbecue," she continued. "Do you like barbecue?"

"Of course."

"The winner of the Springfest barbecue cook-off advances to Memphis in May. The winner of that event is considered the World Champion of Barbecue—or something like that." She was becoming more animated now.

"Really?"

"Yes," she said. "Anyway, Pat came by our concession booth and it turned out that she knew both Randy and me, but separately if you know what I mean?"

"I do."

"Later in the day the three of us walked around looking at the arts and crafts, the military exhibit and the antique tractors. When my son Adam met Randy he really took a liking to him. You know how you can tell when kids like an adult?"

"I think so."

"It's hard for a woman who has a child to meet a nice

man," she went on. "When a man finds out that a woman has a child he runs the other way. Randy wasn't like that. We went out a few times, and then baseball season came along, just as we were beginning to think that there might be something there between us."

A telephone rang in the kitchen and she excused herself. Boulder heard her tell someone that she "would be over in thirty minutes." She returned and said that she needed to leave shortly to go pick up Adam, but that she had a few more minutes.

"Were you and Randy engaged to be married?"

"Oh no," she said. "We were becoming very good friends. Our relationship was heading in that direction, but we weren't there yet. A man would have to sell himself to my son. If Adam didn't like a man I was dating, then I wouldn't think about marriage."

"Maybe that explains why women don't abandon their children like men do," he said.

"That's right," she replied. "Look at all the men who abandon their children. I think they should be—well— you don't want to know what I think." She was changing before Boulder's eyes. No longer was she the portrait of a gentle mother. She was transforming into an angry, agitated woman. Scorn was in her eyes. She raised her right index finger. "A man who will not support his children is not worth living."

"Such a man would get the death sentence if you were on his jury?"

"In a minute."

"Was your husband like that?" Boulder asked.

"He was worse than that. Not only did he fail to provide financial support he never even visited Adam. He deserted Adam and me. I hope he goes to some place where the sun doesn't shine. And the sooner the better." She glanced at a clock on the wall. "Look, I'm sorry, but that's just the way I feel."

"I understand," he said.

"I've got to pick up Adam," she said. "Could you maybe come back in about two hours? I've got something I think you should see."

"Of course," said Boulder.

Boulder returned two hours later and was introduced to Adam Craft, Melinda Craft's twelve-year-old son. He was a sandy-haired, lanky kid who said "sir" in every other sentence. Boulder concluded that she was doing a good job raising this kid.

"Mr. Boulder and I are going to do something on the computer," she told Adam. "I'll come to your room when we finish."

"Okay, Mom."

They went to a small room next to Adam's bedroom. On one side was a computer system laid out on a cheap desk from a discount store. On the other side of the room was an ironing board, folding table and trunk. This was their shared space.

"Randy sent me an email after every game," she said.

"Let me show you." She reached down and turned on the computer. They stood there as it warmed up.

"You've got a fine son," said Boulder.

"Thank you," she replied. "It's not easy, but I've got my parents to help me. They are my babysitters. That's where I went—to pick up Adam."

The computer finally was ready. She sat down in the chair in front of the screen and began typing on the keyboard. She opened an email program then clicked the pointer on an electronic folder for her saved emails. Boulder watched over her shoulder as she opened a folder titled "RC." There was a list of three email messages. She clicked the appropriate places to print them out for Boulder.

"Take a look at these," she said, handing him three sheets of paper.

He studied the first one:

YBYK NJYWCB Y EMMB EYKC RMLGEFR
WMS JMMICB ZCYSRGDSJ QGRRGLE
RFCPC GL RFC QRYLBQ G JMMI
DMPUYPB RM RFC BYW UC AYL
EM NSZJGA ZCQR UGQFCQ

"Obviously, this is some kind of code," Boulder said.
"Yes," she replied.

Boulder looked at the next one:

T RTJE T GYDNM IB
HJOTXU PYD KY UY KY
MTXXBA KYWYAAYR
XTUEK IDK T IBNTBSB
RB HAB MYTXU KEB
ATUEK KETXU FBYFNB
HAB JY CDMUWBXKHN TL PYD
OXYR REHK T WBHX
HMHW TJ H UYYM IYP
HXM H UYYM IHJBIHNN
FNHPBA

He was not a cryptanalyst, but he knew someone who was. He read the third one:

G RFMSEFR MD WMS YJJ
BYW YR UMPI RFC ILMR
GL KW QRMKYAF UGJJ ZCAMKC
SLPYTCJCB UFCL G FMJB WMS

When he finished he looked up at Melinda. She was smiling.

"Randy sent his emails in code because Adam and I both use this computer. He wanted to make certain that I was the only one who read them."

"So you have a key to the code?" asked Boulder.

"Yes, but it's not what you think," she said. "There is a different key for each code." She turned back to the keyboard and began typing. She got on the Internet and went to a website. The site displayed a green baseball field complete with players. There was a large scoreboard in the top left of the screen. The letters to the word WELCOME popped out of home plate one at a time and bounced around the bases. When they returned to home plate they disappeared and the words "Randall's World" appeared in the middle of the screen in large white letters. Underneath that were underlined words that were hyperlinks to other websites and pages on this website. Included in the list were "Baseball Greats, Statistics, My Favorite Players, Great Games, Great Hitters, Great Fielders," and many more. He then noticed more links in the grandstand section of the graphic before him. The links in that section were "Code Breakers, Cryptology, War Codes, Codes in History, Gordian Knot," and several more. It was as impressive a web page as Boulder had ever seen.

"Watch when I click on the scoreboard," she said. She moved the mouse in her right hand until the pointer was over the scoreboard. She clicked and the page changed to a graphic depicting ten baseball players standing side-by-side. Boulder immediately noticed that they were wearing sequential numbers. The first player wore number one, the second player wore number two, and so on. He studied the screen and noticed something else. The player wearing number seven was Mickey Mantle, number eight was Yogi Berra, number nine was Ted Williams and so on. Each player wore the number that he wore during his Major League career. This had to have taken some research or had to have been designed by someone who was a baseball fanatic. Boulder deduced that it was designed by someone who loved both research and baseball.

"I will now click on a player," she said, moving the pointer. She clicked and the page was replaced by the so-called "404" message informing the user that the requested page does not exist. She clicked on the back arrow and returned to the page with the baseball players lined up. She clicked on another player and received the same message. She repeated this procedure until she had clicked on every player and gotten the same message. "This is not the way it was when I did it before."

"What do you mean?" asked Boulder.

"Randy told me to wait until 10:30 on the night after Adam's game, then go to this website. It's Randy's website. I was to click on the scoreboard and that would take me to the page with the baseball players. Then I was to click on the baseball player that wore the number that matched the number of runs that were scored in the top of the sixth inning. When I clicked on that number it gave me the code to decipher the email that he sent me."

"That's an elaborate way to send mail," Boulder said.

"You would have had to know Randy to understand,"

she said. "He was a brilliant but shy man. He was also thinking of Adam when he did this."

"How so?"

"Randy and I had gone out only three times when assignment of the youth baseball teams was held. Randy coached the Brown Properties team. Adam was assigned to his team. Being the sensitive person that he was, as well as knowing how parents can be, Randy felt it best not to go out together until after the season. Otherwise, if he played Adam more than other players some parent might criticize him for being partial to Adam."

"But that happens all the time, doesn't it? Coaches play their own children."

"I know," she said. "But that's the kind of man he was. Maybe that's why I was becoming attracted to him." She lowered her head and paused before continuing. "Anyway, he said that during the season he would send emails. The season was to last only six weeks. The more I thought about it, the more I thought it was kind of cool."

"Did you save any of the keys to the coded messages?"

She got up and went over to the other side of the room. She opened the trunk beside the ironing board and pulled out two sheets of white paper. "Here they are."

Boulder looked at them. The first page was a print-out of what looked like a bull's-eye with only two rings. The outer ring contained the letters of the alphabet in clockwise order around the ring. The inner ring also contained the letters of the alphabet, but they were off-set against the outer ring so that the "a" in the inner circle was under the "c" of the outer circle, the "b" in the inner circle was under the "d" and so on. The second sheet contained the letters of the alphabet in capital letters printed in two columns side-by-side. The alphabet went in order down the left column and then down the right column. Beside each letter was a dash and a small letter of the alphabet. They appeared to be matched in random order. The "A" had an "h" beside it, "B" had and "i" beside it, "C" had a "c" beside it.

"All you have to do is just replace the letter in the email with the letter on the code," she said. She reached in the trunk again and produced a spiral notepad. She opened it to the first page and handed it to him. It contained hand printing. "Here's how the first letter was deciphered."

He looked at the page and read the letter.

Adam played a good game tonight. You looked beautiful sitting there in the stands. I look forward to the day we can go public. Best wishes.

Boulder compared the bull's-eye page and immediately saw the how the code worked. A "y" in the code was really an "a" because the "a" was the letter under the "y" on the inner circle. Clever, yet simple.

"Tell me again. Why did he use coded messages?" Boulder asked.

"It was in case Adam opened my email by mistake," she said. "We share the computer."

"May I have these papers? I'll return them to you."

"I prefer to keep the original, but you can take them down to Main Street Zip Printers and they will make you a copy. Oh, wait. I know how to make you a copy," she said.

She went back to the computer system and placed the pages one-by-one on a scanner. The computer scanned the documents and printed them out. She handed them to Boulder.

"I'm still amazed by computer technology," Boulder said.

He said goodbye to Melinda Craft and her son Adam and then left. He did not notice the green Ford Taurus that followed him from half a block behind.

CHAPTER 16

Boulder drove to the nearest phone booth and called Carson Kelly, a technician at a computer repair store in Jackson. Boulder had met Kelly a year earlier when Boulder's computer system had malfunctioned after lightning struck outside Boulder's condo, followed the telephone wire into his residence and melted parts of his answering machine and computer. His computer would turn on, but the screen was blank even though strange little clicking sounds came from inside. Boulder found a computer repair shop in the telephone book, hauled the system in and was informed that his ". . . motherboard was fried." He spent twenty minutes with Kelly learning more than he would ever understand about things that could be recovered from computer files. He learned that clicking on "Delete" meant that things were just moved to somewhere else in the computer. A good technician could recover almost anything that had ever been in a computer. Unfortunately, in Boulder's lightning strike case there would be no recovery, only a lesson learned in the need to back up files on a daily basis.

Kelly and Boulder found each other likable and interesting. Kelly, who at twenty-two was half Boulder's age, was fascinated with Boulder's private-eye life, especially with the aspect of putting together a puzzle to solve a case. He was also an amateur cryptanalyst. Boulder assured him that detective work was more about verifying statements that people made and checking out mundane details than it was solving a mysterious puzzle. Nevertheless, Kelly was intrigued and asked question after question with the enthusiasm of a ten-year-old boy on his first fishing trip. Boulder was also interested in Kelly and his work. Boulder wanted to know more about computers. Even though he had a state-of-the art system in his office/bedroom he felt that he was getting left behind on the technology highway. He was adept at using the Internet for research purposes, but did not know as much as he should about digital cameras, videos and other new computer accessories.

Kelly represented the modern American employee, a person interested in his field of work more than who his employer might be. Kelly said that it did not matter whom he worked for as long as he could work on computers.

"Heck, I've changed employers three times in the last year and a half, but I haven't changed jobs, if you know what I mean," he said.

Hardly a week went by that someone did not come into the repair shop to ask Kelly if he would like to go to work for a larger company. Kelly turned them all down.

"I like building computers and finding out what makes these things go down," he said. "Computers are a lot simpler than most people think they are."

Kelly built a computer for Boulder. A month later Boulder called on Kelly to help solve a case in which data needed to be retrieved from a stolen floppy disk. Boulder concluded it was time to use Kelly again.

"Are you interested in helping me with another case?" asked Boulder in a telephone call to Kelly.

"Man, am I ever," Kelly said enthusiastically. "What's up?"

"I need to take a look at the files inside a computer, but I can't get past the password screen when I turn on the computer."

"That's easy," Kelly said. "But I need to come over and do it myself. I can't tell you on the telephone."

"Can you come to Southaven?"

"Where is that?" Kelly asked.

"About three and a half hours north of Jackson," said Boulder. "Right at the top of Mississippi. I can make it worth your time."

"Are we going to break into a system?"

"You've been reading too many mysteries," Boulder said. "We have permission from the next of kin."

"Does that mean there has been a murder?"

"Don't sound so enthusiastic," said Boulder. "Yes, there has been a murder."

"I can take off tomorrow," Kelly said.

"Take the Stateline Road exit off Interstate 55. I'll meet you at the library," Boulder said and gave more explicit directions. "Be there at noon. I'll be inside."

CHAPTER 17

Using the key that Randy Crowley's stepmother had given him, Boulder and Kelly entered the apartment of the victim around noon on Wednesday. Kelly carried a computer bag loaded with equipment and a laptop.

The living room furniture consisted of a leather sofa, matching chair, coffee table strewn with sports and computer magazines and a large screen television. The walls were bare. In the adjoining dining room, a black laptop computer and several shiny compact discs sat on a plain table. Boulder walked in the kitchen and opened the refrigerator to find old containers of ketchup, mustard and mayonnaise. In the garbage can were wrappers from fast food restaurants and a cardboard box from a home delivery pizza restaurant. Randy led the take-out food life common to a college student.

They moved to a bedroom that was more nicely furnished. Boulder checked the closet and found one navy blue blazer, a pair of gray slacks and three oxford dress shirts. In the dresser drawers he discovered a large collection of Polo shirts, jeans and slacks. In the second bedroom they found a motherlode of computer equipment, an expensive stereo system and a collection of music CDs. On the walls were posters of baseball stadiums.

Kelly sat down in front of the monitor and turned on

the computer as Boulder told him about the emails to Melinda and about Randy's website. Shortly, a box appeared on the screen instructing the user to "Please enter username and password."

"How do you get past that?" said Boulder.

"Let's see what I have in my toolkit," Kelly said as he reached down into his bag and pulled out a screwdriver. He used it to remove the cover from the computer. He bent down and reached behind the computer. The screen showed a few static lines like on old television set. Kelly said, "Um hmm," to himself several times, then finally sat back in the chair. He typed "Kilroy" in the username box on the screen and "washere" in the password box, the latter box showing only "*******." He tapped the "enter" key and the computer began whirring as the username box disappeared.

"How did you do that?" Boulder asked. "I thought a person couldn't get in without a password."

"Ask me no questions and I'll tell you no lies," Kelly replied.

"Seriously. I didn't know that was possible," said Boulder. "I thought if something in a computer was password protected that nobody else could get into it."

"Assume that anything is possible when it comes to information in a computer," said Kelly.

"What did you do? I want to know."

"If you must know, there is a little battery inside that keeps certain things stored in case there is a power failure," explained Kelly. "If the battery gets removed then replaced, the computer thinks it's time to start all over again."

"So it thinks you're Randy Crowley?"

"It doesn't think anything," Kelly said. "It just has to reset some settings if the power fails and there is no backup. I chose a random username and password."

"Son of a gun," said Boulder.

The screen changed to dark blue and small icon images lined up across the top of the screen like those on hundreds of thousands of other personal computers. One of the icons represented an email program. Kelly clicked on it and the email screen appeared. He selected the SENT folder and opened it. Boulder stood behind him watching over his shoulder. There were three emails sent to Melinda Craft in June. Kelly clicked on the one with the earliest date and up came the coded text.

"This is the first one, I presume," said Kelly. "The code idea is cool, although rather basic. He's using a Cesar Cipher with this one. That's where the letters of the alphabet are on the outside of a wheel, and then a smaller wheel is offset inside of the outside wheel. A person just looks at a letter on a wheel and sees which letter is under it."

"Is there an email that was sent out last Wednesday?" Boulder asked, remembering the circles on one of the printouts he got from Melinda Craft.

"Don't see anything in the outbox waiting to be sent. Let's check out his website. Here's his website creation program." He said as he clicked away. "And here are the files in his website program. Man, this guy has some kind of good website."

"Do you find anything that gives the codes on the scoreboard?" asked Boulder.

"Yes," Kelly replied. "Here's the page with the scoreboard. The numbers all have hyperlinks to the same page. Let's go there and check it out." He clicked and a new page appeared. It had a table of thirty-one numbers in a box just like a calendar. At the top of the page it told the user, i.e. Melinda, to click on her day of birth.

"Randy-Boy is adding another layer to the puzzle. Someone who didn't know her birthday would have to go through thirty-one possibilities to get the code," Kelly said. "This might take some time, but it can be done in a couple of hours."

"I'll just call Melinda and ask her for her date of birth," Boulder said.

He went to the kitchen and picked up the telephone receiver. Three minutes later he returned. A serious look masked his face.

"I called her home and got no answer, so I called the Kroger store," Boulder said. "She didn't show up for work today."

CHAPTER 18

"What are you going to do?" Carson Kelly asked. "Do you think she has been kidnapped?"

"Resist the temptation to jump to conclusions," Boulder said. "But I would like to check Melinda Craft's house just to see if her car is there."

"Wait just a minute. I think I've found something. There are not thirty-one different hyperlinks here. Well, technically, there are thirty-one. But all thirty-one are to the same web address. Everyone of them is the same."

"Meaning?" asked Boulder.

"That there is only one code. No matter which day is clicked on it takes you to the same code. Very interesting," he explained as he clicked some more. "And here it is. This code uses a number OR a letter for each letter of the alphabet. I like it."

On the screen was displayed the following:

A-7-U	G-21-A	M-1-G	S-13-M	Y-19-S
B-8-V	H-22-B	N-2-H	T-14-N	Z-20-T
C-9-W	I-23-C	O-3-I	O-3-I	U-15-O
D-10-X	J-24-O	P-4-O	P-4-5	V-16-P
E-11-Y	K-25-E	O-5-K	W-17-Q	
F-12-Z	L-26-F	R-6-L	X-18-R	

USE NUMBER *OR* LETTER, BUT NOT BOTH

"How does it work?" Boulder asked.

"Give me a word," Kelly said.

"Computer," said Boulder.

"Good. Now take a look at the code." Boulder leaned forward and squinted as Kelly continued explaining, "The C could be either a 9 or a W, the O could be a 3 or an I and the M could be a 1 or a G. Thus, nine, three, one, four, fifteen, fourteen, eleven, six would spell COMPUTER or W, I, G, J, O, N, Y, L would spell COMPUTER. There could be—let's see—lots of combinations that would spell the word computer."

"Okay," Boulder said slowly, wondering where this was going.

"In other words, if somebody got this email without the code it would take him or her some time to decipher it, depending on the skill level of the code breaker," explained Kelly. "I think Randy-Boy was protecting the message from more than just a twelve-year-old boy."

"But you said there was no email message with that particular code?" Boulder asked.

"I'm saying that there is no email in the SENT box or the TO BE SENT box," Kelly said.

"Can a person delete stuff from a SENT box?" Boulder asked.

"Oh, sure. Let me do some checking here." He said as he typed on the keyboard for a minute, and then announced, "There was no email sent from this computer to Melinda's email address last Wednesday, period.

I checked the trash and other files where it could be on this machine."

"It was probably another love letter anyway," Boulder said.

"Unless . . ."

"Unless what?" asked Boulder.

"Unless Randy composed it first, planning on sending it later. If that were the case, it would be in the DRAFTS file. Let me check." He clicked and typed some more. "Not there either." Kelly stroked his chin, and then snapped his fingers. "Just because he didn't send it doesn't mean he didn't write it," Kelly said.

"Meaning?"

"Let's check his word processor. He might have written it first, then planned to paste it into the email message to his lady friend." Again, Kelly tapped away. "I think we may have something here. His other emails are here. Yes, here's the one I think you are looking for. It's dated last Wednesday. Let's open it and see what it says." More tapping on the keyboard. "There you are." Kelly turned around and smiled proudly at Boulder.

The detective looked at the monitor and was not amused. "It's in that letter-number code."

"I know," Kelly said. "But I think I know where the key can be found."

"Really?"

Kelly's fingers went to work on the keyboard. He closed out the word processing program and opened up

Crowley's website design program. Crowley's website and a file bar appeared on the screen. Kelly found the pages that connected to the hyperlinks on the baseball players' uniforms. He opened each one and studied it.

"Well, I'll be a monkey's uncle," he said exhaling.

"What is it?" asked Boulder.

"This code is the same for every day," said Kelly.

"I don't get it," Boulder said. "You've lost me."

"No matter which player number she clicked on it would link her to the same code. This guy wasn't taking any chances," explained Kelly. "No matter what the score was in the top of the sixth inning she was going to receive the same message last Wednesday night. This guy was making sure she got THIS message."

"Can you tell what the email says?"

"He's using another random code," Kelly said. "But it's consistent with the way he did the other one. Can you get me a paper and pen?"

Boulder looked around and found a three-ring notebook and a pencil and handed them to Kelly, who started writing. After fifteen minutes he handed the deciphered message to Boulder.

There is something terrible about to happen at work. It's all about the janitors' insurance. If anything happens to me don't let First Thursday take place. Life and death matter. I love you.

Boulder and Kelly looked at each other for a minute, attempting to analyze and comprehend the message.

"There is something here that has to do with Randy Crowley's death," Boulder said.

Kelly sat in the chair and Boulder remained standing, both in thought again. Suddenly a telephone on a table beside them rang. They jerked at the same time, and collided with each other.

CHAPTER 19

At the end of the second ring an answering machine under the telephone clicked on. They could hear the voice clearly.

"This is Randy. I can't come to the phone so leave a message. I might call you back." Then the beep sounded, followed by the click of someone on the other end hanging up. They stood up and moved apart, embarrassment from the fright fading into curiosity.

Boulder took a step to the machine and studied it. He pressed a button and the messages began. Each was preceded by an electronic voice announcing the date and time.

"Wednesday. 11:40 p.m." There was no message. Only background noise.

"Thursday. 8:40 a.m."

"Randall, this is Jenny at the office. Ed wants to know if you're coming to work today. You are supposed to call in if you're sick, remember."

"Friday. 9:12 p.m."

"Hi Randy. It's Dad." There was the sound of sniffling and crying. "I just wanted to hear your voice. Oh, my God. You can't be gone."

"Saturday. 6:15 p.m." said the machine voice. Then a female voice.

"Good evening Mr. Crowley this is Barbara with

Resorts International. I'm calling to let you know that you are a winner. Please call one, eight hundred, five, five, five, two thousand to receive your claim number. Have a wonderful day."

There were no more messages. Boulder played them again and cocked his head as he listened intently.

"What was the background noise in that first message?" Boulder asked.

"I couldn't tell," Kelly said.

"Listen very closely," said Boulder. "I'll turn up the volume." They listened again.

"Sounds like cars coming and going," Kelly said.

"You're right. There's something else in the background. Listen again."

Boulder played it again.

"Two-way radios? Taxicabs, maybe?" Kelly asked.

"Radio, for sure. Not taxicabs," said Boulder. "Cops."

"You think someone was in a phone booth in the police parking lot?" Kelly asked.

"Possible."

"It might be someone on a cell phone at a scene where cars are coming and going and police are talking on their radios."

"That's exactly what it sounds like," Boulder said. "And I know what was going on in Southaven last Wednesday night at 11:40."

"What?"

"That's when I got picked up at Randy Crowley's murder scene."

Kelly's eyes grew larger. "You got arrested for murder?"

"Let's just say that I got picked up on suspicion of murder," said Boulder.

"Cool."

"No. Not cool. I need to find out who killed Randy Crowley so that I can totally clear my name."

"Randy Crowley being the dude that lived in this apartment?" asked Kelly.

"Yes."

"Mind if I do a little more poking around in his computer?"

"Help yourself," Boulder said. "His stepmother said we could look at anything we wanted. While you are doing that, I'm going to check out the rest of this place."

Kelly sat back down and began working at the computer. Boulder went room by room in search of anything that might help lead to why someone would want to kill Randy. He found nothing of interest. He returned to the bedroom where Kelly was working.

"I think I might have found something," said Kelly. "Crowley forwarded some stuff from the office to himself using email. I'll let you look and see if there is anything interesting."

Boulder looked over Kelly's shoulder at the emails. There were seven. Four contained links to baseball websites, one was a notice of the coming First Thursday meeting, one was an email from the chamber of commerce reminding members to attend a recreation committee meeting and one was a message that read "The attached is the reason." The attachment to the last email was an employment agreement between SVN Technologies and Randy. It appeared to have been scanned and then attached. It was four pages of small type.

"Would you like these printed out?" Kelly asked.

"Yes."

As they waited for the printing to finish Kelly said, "It may be nothing, but there is something you should know."

"What's that?"

"Crowley's Internet Service Provider was SVNMS Net. Isn't that where he worked?"

"Yes. SVN Technology Services of Mississippi."

"Right," Kelly said. "It's possible that someone there could have read his email."

"Like those messages to Melinda Craft?" asked Boulder.

"Yep. His messages probably went right through their server. Someone at the company who had access could read them with no problem."

"Do you think Crowley would have known that was possible?" Boulder asked.

"He was a website designer and a network technician," said Kelly. "There was no way he could not have known that."

"That would explain it then."

"Explain what?" asked Kelly.

"Why Crowley sent his messages in code to Melinda Craft," Boulder said. "He told her that it was because he didn't want her son to read them. Maybe it was because he didn't want his employer reading them."

"From the looks of that last email message that he never sent to her, I would say that he thought something was about to happen at the company," said Kelly.

"Of course," Boulder said. "But what?"

"The answer might be in these messages that he sent to himself," said Kelly.

"You are probably right," Boulder said. "I need to have a lawyer look at them. Would you mind delivering these to a lawyer in Jackson for me?"

"Sure."

"Her name is Laura Webster. I'll write down her address and phone number for you," said Boulder. "I'll let her know you are coming. It would be good if you could drop them off at her house in Jackson today."

"Consider it done."

Boulder picked up the documents from the printer. He reached in his pocket and pulled out two $100 bills. "Here's a down payment on your services. Is $500 satisfactory with you?"

"I'll say," said Kelly.

"I'll send you $300 more when I get back to Jackson," said Boulder. "Your service has been very helpful, Carson. I never could have found this by myself."

"Can't I stick around and help you with the case some more? You never know when you might need a computer guy."

"I'm afraid not," Boulder said. "I'll call you if I need you."

They walked together to the front door of the apartment and shook hands. Kelly got in his car and drove away. Boulder felt that there was something else in the apartment that he had missed. He walked back in, leaving the front door open. As he got to the hallway the telephone rang. Boulder listened as the answering machine gave its message. Then from the speaker on the machine he heard something that put a knot in his stomach and made the hair on his neck stand up.

"Boulder," said a whispered male voice. "I would get out of there right now if I were you."

CHAPTER 20

Instinct told Jack Boulder to flee. He resisted the impulse, knowing that someone was surely watching the front door to Randy's apartment, waiting for him to emerge. He wondered what would happen if he went outside. Would he be confronted? Would he be shot by the same person who shot Randy? Was the call a warning? He considered the possibility that there might be an explosive device in the apartment and that the call was a warning to get out of the building.

Eventually he decided that the call was indeed a warning, a warning letting him know that he was being watched while in Southaven. Two could play at this game. He dialed the number of the Southaven Police Department and asked to speak to Officer Worthmore.

"She's unavailable. Would you like to leave a message?"

"Yes," said Boulder. The next thing he heard was Worthmore's voicemail requesting that the caller leave a message and that she would call back.

Boulder left a message for her. "This is Jack Boulder. If you receive this message before 2:00 call me back." He gave the number of the telephone he was calling from. He thought about calling back to the police department and asking them to respond, but he realized immediately that he did not want to explain why he was in the apartment of the person he was charged with murdering.

The phone rang. His heart skipped a beat, but he recovered fast enough to answer it before it could ring a second time.

"Yes," he said.

"Is that you, Boulder?" It was the voice of Officer Worthmore.

"It is," he answered.

"What's up?" she asked.

"I'm in Randy Crowley's apartment. His mother gave me the key. But I think someone is watching me. I received a call on this telephone telling me to get out," Boulder said. "Would you be available for a drive-through of the parking lot?"

"I'm off-duty. My voicemail automatically pages me."

"Oh."

"Watch for my car," Officer Worthmore said. "What's the address?" He gave it to her. "Am I supposed to be on the lookout for someone in particular?"

"All I have is a voice," he said.

Twelve minutes later, Boulder peeked through the blinds and saw her blue Camaro pull into the parking lot outside. She nestled into a parking place, looked around, then got out and went to the front door of the apartment. She wore a pair of khaki cargo shorts and a dark blue shirt. A handbag that looked like it came from L.L. Bean hung from a strap draped over her shoulder.

Boulder opened the door and let her in. He went to the window and peered through the blinds just in time to see a green Ford Taurus pull out from a space and leave. He could not make out the driver, but he was able to see the tag number. He turned and all but shouted it to the police officer. She immediately pulled a cell phone from her bag and punched in a number.

"This is Worthmore. I need a twenty-eight," she barked. She gave the tag number and told the other party to call her on her cell phone.

"Thanks for responding," Boulder said. "Whoever is in that car has either been watching this apartment or following me."

"What are you doing here?"

"Randall Crowley, Jr.'s stepmother offered me a reward to find her stepson's killer." Officer Worthmore looked away and squinted her forehead as she processed this information.

"So what did you find?" she asked.

Before Boulder could answer, the cell phone in Worthmore's hand started beeping. She answered it and listened intently. She nodded her head, said thanks and returned the device to her handbag.

"That green Ford Taurus that just left the parking lot is owned by Bull's-Eye Security," she said.

CHAPTER 21

Officer Worthmore and Boulder sat down at the dining room table, each staring away into unfocused space.

"They have probably been following you since you got out of jail," Officer Worthmore said.

"Or they could have been staking out this apartment just to see who came here," Boulder said.

"Why would they do that?"

"Perhaps Crowley's stepmother hired Bull's-Eye just like she hired me." As he said the words he thought of Laura's admonition and caution that he had not exactly been hired by Mrs. Hogan-Crowley. He decided that this was not relevant to the situation at hand anyway, because he had just told Worthmore that he had been offered a reward.

"On the other hand, why would she hire somebody if Southaven's finest had already arrested somebody—namely me—for her stepson's murder?" asked Boulder.

"Maybe she doesn't believe you did it," Officer Worthmore said.

Boulder thought back to his meeting with Hogan-Crowley and agreed that this made sense.

"You don't believe I did it either, do you?"

"No," she replied. "I already told you. People who just committed crimes don't run toward the scene, they run away."

"That's true in most cases," Boulder said. "But an arsonist will often be in the crowd watching the building that he set on fire burn down. That's when he gets his real thrill."

"You keep using the 'he' word," Officer Worthmore said.

"Have you ever heard of a female arsonist?" he asked.

"I can't really say that I have," she said.

"Your point is well-taken though. I need to be more sensitive about how I talk," Boulder said. "It's just that men commit almost all the crimes."

"How long have you been retired?" Officer Worthmore asked.

"Almost four years," he said.

"I've got some news for you. Society is changing fast. Women are getting involved in more and more criminal activity," she said. "They are still being victimized like crazy and always will. But things are changing."

"Why did you get into law enforcement?" Boulder asked.

"It runs in my family's blood. My older brother is on the Memphis P. D. and my father was in law enforcement all his life in DeSoto county. He was sheriff until he retired a few years ago."

"I heard something about a nasty campaign a few years back that involved Harold Haggard. Was your father part of that?" he asked.

"Who told you that?" she snapped.

"Jefferson Stallman."

"None of that is true," she said, her voice rising and her face turning crimson. "My father was a good man. He never ran around on my mother. Those pictures were faked, and everybody knows it. Harold Haggard would have done anything to defeat my father."

"Including murder?" Boulder asked.

"Yes. Including murder," she answered.

"You really don't like Haggard, do you?"

"No I don't," she said forcefully. "And you won't find anyone in DeSoto county who likes him either."

"You would like to see him involved somehow with Randy Crowley's death, wouldn't you?"

She turned and looked Boulder straight in his eyes and said, "Damn right."

"But you really don't believe that, do you?"

"I have no specific evidence if that's what you mean," she answered. "But wouldn't you agree that it was very coincidental that he appeared on the scene at just the time you were standing over the body?"

Boulder suddenly snapped his fingers and said, "It just dawned on me. Of course."

"What are you talking about?" she asked.

"Worthmore, you may be right!" She leaned forward as he spelled it out. "I did not hear a car just drive up. I heard a car racing up. I heard tires squealing when

Haggard turned off Getwell Road onto the road to the baseball fields," Boulder said. "That's not the way a security guard or a law enforcement officer would approach two cars on the side of the road late at night. He would have approached cautiously."

"That's for sure," she agreed.

"You are right," he said. "I was set up."

CHAPTER 22

Boulder felt a vibration from his pager. He studied the display and saw a number that he did not recognize.

"Is 662 your local area code?" he asked.

"Yes," she replied, and handed him her cell phone. "Want to make a call?"

"Thanks." He began dialing the number displayed on his pager, then stopped and said, "It might not be a good idea to use your phone. There will be a record of the call. Who knows? It might be a set-up of some kind. I don't want you to get into trouble. I appreciate what you are doing to help me even if it might be for the wrong reason. Remember, I'm a murder suspect as far as your employer is concerned."

"Good point," she conceded.

Boulder used the telephone in the kitchen. A man answered.

"This is Jack Boulder returning your call."

"This is Randall Crowley. I got your pager number from Mr. Stallman's office."

"What can I do for you?" asked Boulder.

"I overheard your conversation with my wife and I don't think she is telling the whole truth. I regret to have to say this, but I think she may have had something to do with Randy's death."

"In what way?" Boulder asked.

"I don't know, but she was very jealous of him. I'm afraid I made a real mess of our marriage because of it. We had an argument two weeks ago, and she said that our marriage would be fine if Randy wasn't around all the time. They resented each other very much."

"Do you have any evidence?"

"No," Crowley, Sr. answered. "Just a hunch."

"Was there any insurance on your son?"

"Not enough to kill him over. Between Ruth and me, we have more than enough money to last a lifetime. I've got to go now. Ruth went to pick up our dog at the DeSoto County Animal Clinic. I hope it isn't true, but she might be involved and I thought you should know."

Boulder hung up the telephone, turned toward Officer Worthmore, and said, "That was Crowley, Sr., telling me that he thinks his wife might have something to do with his son's murder."

"She has enough money to hire someone to have it done," Officer Worthmore said.

"Thanks for coming by," Boulder said.

"No problem," she said. "Now we at least know this murder was not some random act. Someone is still involved and wants you out of town."

"And I'm beginning to think that someone is Harold Haggard."

"Here's my cell phone number," she said, handing him a business card. "I'm working swing shift tonight. Call me if you need me."

CHAPTER 23

First Thursday was obviously something that had concerned Randy Crowley. Boulder thought about the meeting and recalled that a company jet made the rounds and picked up the district managers and landed at a nearby airport late Wednesday afternoon. He decided that he would try to be there when the airplane landed. He called Jamie Whatley, Randy's co-worker who had told him about the plane, and learned that it usually landed between 6:30 and 7:30 p.m. at the Olive Branch airport. It would be easy to spot because it had SVN Tech painted on the side. Whatley wasn't sure what kind of plane it was, but it had to be big enough to hold ten people.

After consulting the DeSoto county road map that he had obtained from the Southaven Chamber of Commerce, Boulder headed east on Goodman Road and drove about ten miles until he reached Hacks Cross Road. There he turned north, drove past Holiday Inn University Drive, which led to a conference and retreat center, and turned right onto the road leading into the Olive Branch airport. Located less than twenty-five miles from downtown Memphis, the facility was a busy site for a general aviation airport. The 6,000-foot runway was long enough to accommodate many types of business and pleasure aircraft.

Boulder drove to the most crowded part of the parking lot and found a vacant space between two large SUVs. It was just the spot he was looking for to hide, or at least make inconspicuous, the readily identifiable Camaro. He did not know how long he would have to wait or even if he was already too late. He got out and walked over to a spot where he could see the aircraft parked on the ramp. All he knew was that he was looking for a business jet with "SVN Tech" painted on the side in royal blue letters.

A gentle relief of a breeze blew in from the south as he watched a small, two-seater plane land out on the runway. It taxied to a point not far from him and a man and teenage girl crawled out. The man talked to her for a few minutes, sometimes making turning gestures with his right hand, then gave her a congratulatory handshake. She grinned and walked proudly toward the parking lot. The man went to a building that had a "Learn to fly" sign on the door.

A few more planes landed as the sun began to set behind him, casting long shadows across the runway. He looked into the sky toward the east and noticed a white business jet enter the landing pattern. It lowered its gear and moved north as it slowly descended. There was something written on its side, but Boulder couldn't make it out. The sleek aircraft made a sweeping left turn onto its base approach then another left turn onto final approach. Boulder squinted but was still unable to make out the markings. Boulder's wristwatch beeped its hourly electronic chime as the plane touched down on runway 18. The gleam of the sunlight glowed a light gold on the top of the fuselage as it slowed down and rolled to a stop directly out in front of Boulder. He saw it clearly now. "SVN Tech" was painted on the side of the airplane, just above the windows.

The Cessna Citation Sovereign taxied onto the ramp and parked in front of a hangar to Boulder's left. He heard the whine of the jet engines fade to a stop. The door opened as a large van/truck, like the ones used by rental car companies to shuttle passengers at airports, pulled out onto the ramp and parked near the plane. Nine men and one woman walked out of the plane, ducking their heads at the threshold step as if bowing to Mother Earth. They were dressed in business casual. The driver of the van opened the cargo door of the aircraft, removed luggage and placed it in the back of the van. Boulder counted eleven bags. The passengers climbed up into the van and it drove toward the parking lot.

Boulder suddenly realized that the van would be down the road before he could get to his car. He turned and sprinted toward the parking lot. He stopped immediately and changed his pace to a fast walk. In today's world, someone running on airport property was cause for suspicion and investigation. As he approached his car, he muttered a mild curse as the van was already turning onto the main road. His mild curse turned into a major curse as he reached his car and discovered a flat tire on his right front wheel. When he realized that his car was parked too close to the adjacent SUV to change the flat, he kicked the tire and uttered a loud grunt that came from the depths of his stomach.

He put his hands on his hips and considered the situation. The night was taking over the day. The worst-case scenario would be that the SUV beside the Camaro was owned by someone who was away on a trip. The best-case scenario would be that the owner would walk up within the next thirty seconds and drive away leaving Boulder plenty of space to change the flat tire. He walked around to the rear of the SUV and saw that it displayed a Tennessee license plate.

As Boulder pondered his next move, he saw a car drive into the parking lot. He tensed as in the fading light of dusk he read what was displayed on the driver's side door of the Crowne Victoria. It read "Bull's-Eye Security of Mississippi." Boulder stepped back between the SUV and the Camaro and watched as the car pulled into a nearby parking space. The door opened and a tall man in his late fifties got out and glanced around before closing his door. He wore a khaki security company uniform with a gold stripe down each leg and a gold patch on each sleeve. He was over six feet tall and had a shaved head. In his left hand he carried a black, soft leather briefcase. Boulder watched as he walked down the backside of the hangar, then out onto the ramp where the Citation was parked for the night, chocks already under its wheels. The man in the security uniform reached up and inserted a key, then rotated his hand. Boulder moved several cars down the parking aisle so that he could get a better look. The man was no longer there. Boulder thought he saw movement in the cockpit. Less than a minute later the man walked down the stair door of the airplane, then closed it and locked it. The black briefcase was still in his hand. He walked military-style back to the Crowne Victoria and drove away, talking on a cell phone as he did so.

CHAPTER 24

There is an old story about a delivery truck that attempted to go under a low viaduct but got wedged underneath because the truck was too tall. The driver, several passers-by and even the local fire department tried in vain to get the truck unstuck from its position. Just as they were about to give up, a small boy rode up on his bicycle and said, "Bet you're going to let some air out of the tires now and drive it out, huh?"

Jack Boulder thought of that story, realizing that he was overcomplicating his flat tire situation. Even though the SUV was too close beside the Camaro to change the tire, his car was not blocked in. He got in the car, cranked it up and drove forward five feet. He then got out and, with plenty of operating room, changed the tire.

He sat back down in his car and thought about what he had just seen. Someone from Bull's-Eye Security, probably Harold Haggard, went onboard the SVN Tech plane. He had a key to the plane. He probably left something from the black bag on the plane. What was wrong with this picture?

Perhaps Bull's-Eye was employed by SVN Tech and was simply delivering something to the plane. Boulder wished that he could have used a scanner to listen to the cell phone call as the security company owner drove out of the parking lot. A few years ago Boulder had an array of scanners and listening devices. He destroyed them after the Mississippi Legislature passed a law in 1999 making it illegal to intercept a cell phone conversation. Such scanners and listening devices were still around, but it was a fool who would use one. Current penalty for such conduct was six moths in jail and a $1,000 fine. Nevertheless, distributors from foreign countries still offered the equipment to unscrupulous buyers.

Boulder decided to drive to the SVN Tech building just because he did not have a better strategy. As he drove by the conference center he noticed the bus that had picked up the SVN Tech passengers was parked in its designated space near the front door. He pulled in and drove slowly around the parking lot, alert for the Bull's-Eye Security car. He found no sign of it.

He cruised back down Goodman Road toward Southaven. When he came to Getwell Road he turned left and drove toward the lighted glow of Snowden Grove Park. It was an Americana scene at its finest: Baseball fields flooded with light from overhead; parents and friends yelling encouragement to young baseball players; cracks and pops of baseball bats connecting with balls; the aroma of fresh popcorn mingled with the smell of freshly-cut grass; vehicles driving in and out of the large parking lot; and shouts of "good game" and "see you at practice."

Boulder drove slowly through the parking lot savoring it all. He stopped at the concession stand and bought a snow cone and a T-shirt. He drove out to the spot where he found the body a week ago and began asking questions of himself.

Why would someone kill a youth baseball coach? Why was Harold Haggard at the park that night? Why was someone from Bull's-Eye Security inside the SVN plane? What did Randy Crowley discover that would make him think his life was in danger? These and many more questions shuffled around inside Boulder's head.

CHAPTER 25

As Boulder sat in his car pondering questions that needed answers, he felt his pager vibrate. He checked and recognized Laura's telephone number. He went back to the concession area at Snowden Grove and called her.

"The employment contract you sent is most intriguing," she said. "I've closed real estate loans that had mortgages with fewer paragraphs."

Boulder listened as she discussed the complexity of the documents. Behind him, he heard the crack of a bat hitting a ball and the cheer of the crowd.

"You said that you got this from Crowley's computer files?" she asked.

"That's right."

"What else did you get from his computer?" Laura asked.

"We looked at several emails that were sent to his girlfriend Melinda Craft. We looked around in his files for sure. We did have permission from his stepmother. The only things I made copies of were the agreement you have and some other emails."

"Do you have those with you?" she asked.

"They are over in the car. I can go get them."

"Please do."

Boulder went to the Camaro and retrieved the papers. Laura had him read them to her word-for-word.

Afterwards, Boulder could sense her mind at work.

"You do work for insurance companies?" she asked.

"You know I do," he said.

"Ever heard of something called key man insurance?" Laura asked.

"Yes. It's a policy the company takes out on its executives, isn't it?"

"That's right," she said. "Have you ever heard of janitors insurance?"

"Now that you mention it," he replied, "Randy said something about janitors insurance in one of his emails. What is it?"

"Janitors insurance is a term used when a corporation takes out life insurance on its regular employees, not just its key executives," she explained.

Boulder stood waiting for more information as the crowd noise at another field rose, wondering how Laura's information was relevant to the case at hand.

"Corporate-owned life insurance, or C-O-L-I as it is referred to in the trade, is life insurance on a company's employees, its retirees and in some cases the spouses and children of employees. The beneficiary is the company that the person worked for," she explained. "Until a few years ago companies were not allowed to take out insurance on regular employees, such as clerks, laborers and janitors because the company was said not to have what is called an insurable interest. In other words, the company could easily replace most employees if one of them died. For example, if the janitor died, how long do you think it would take a company to replace the janitor?"

"A day or two at the most," Boulder said.

"Right. Therefore, the company would not really lose anything or be hurt if the janitor died," Laura said.

"Okay," he said, still wondering where the conversation was leading to.

"On the other hand, if an important executive who made policy decisions and possessed a wealth of knowledge about the company and its critical internal matters died, it could be a devastating blow to the company," she said. "How long would such a person take to replace?"

"It would be weeks or months," Boulder answered.

"Now you know why many companies had so-called key man, or key executive, insurance policies on their top people. It's a wise thing to do in my opinion," Laura said.

"Do we know what kind of policies SVN Tech had?" Boulder asked.

"Not at this point," Laura replied. "But we do know that their employment agreement gave them the right to take out life insurance on the employee in any amount deemed necessary by the management of the company. The clause is buried in the small print of this employment contract. I would wager that ninety-eight percent of the people who signed this agreement are not aware of what it says."

"Do you think website designers would have life insurance contracts on them?" he asked.

"I wouldn't think so, but who knows," Laura said. "This agreement lets the company decide."

"Let me tell you about the rest of my day," he said. He then told her about the call from the father, more about Randy's apartment, the meeting with Officer Worthmore. "I just came from the Olive Branch airport where I saw someone from Bull's-Eye Security put something on the company jet."

"You're kidding," Laura said. "This might be getting serious then. There is something else you should know. SVN Technologies is on the verge of bankruptcy. My intern has been doing the financial research and discovered that the banks have called in their loans."

"Sounds like a motive," Boulder said.

"Jack, what do you think Haggard placed on that airplane?"

"I don't know, but it's got to be checked out. I don't have enough to go to the FBI, and I'm certainly not going to call Ed McGreely."

"I was planning on driving up to Southaven tomorrow to visit Jefferson Stallman," Laura said. "I'll page you when I get there and we can try to sort this out."

"Good," Boulder said. "In the meantime I'm going to meet with Officer Worthmore when she finishes her shift tonight and see if I can find out if the police department is having any better luck."

CHAPTER 26

Boulder remained at the public telephone at Snowden Grove Park and made a call to Officer Worthmore's cell phone. She answered on the first ring.

"I need to tell you something in person," Boulder said.

"We will have to meet after I get off work," she said. "I'm tied up on an escort detail until 11:00. It's just after 8:00 now. Meet me in the parking lot in front of City Hall at 11:45."

"I'll be there," he said.

He spent the next two hours watching baseball games, then drove by the rental house to freshen up. At 11:30 p.m. he drove to city hall and parked headfirst in a space in front of the building. He could see the police department only a half block to the north. Several cars left the police parking lot, no doubt occupied by officers who had just completed their shifts. At 11:50 p.m. he noticed Worthmore's Camaro exit the lot and head his way. She pulled in beside him and got out of her car. She had on police trousers and a loose khaki shirt with rolled-up sleeves.

"Let's go for a walk," she said. "It's too open out here." They turned and walked down a trail into Saucier Park. "Have you ever been down here?"

"Not yet," he replied.

"It's hard to tell at night, but this is one of the most beautiful places in Southaven," Officer Worthmore explained. "My high school class had its class picture taken here. People even come here for weddings. There's a lake over there. Melinda's son Adam caught a string of catfish at the fishing rodeo last month."

They walked around the lake, enough light to see provided by the street lights in the city hall parking lot.

"So what happened since I saw you last?" she asked.

"I went to the airport at Olive Branch and watched the SVN Tech jet land," Boulder answered. She did not say anything and they kept walking. "After everybody got off the plane, I observed a tall, bald-headed man who arrived in a Bull's-Eye Security car open the cabin door with a key and go into the cockpit. I think he left something inside the plane."

"Probably a bomb," she said sarcastically. "That description fits Harold Haggard."

"That's not beyond the realm of possibility, you know. The victim overheard Haggard and McGreely talking about making something look like an accident. Then there is the janitors insurance thing," he said and explained what Laura had told him about the subject. "How is the department's case coming?"

"We're looking at McGreely of course, but also the stepmother. She may have hired a hit man. She has plenty of money and apparently is ruthless enough. She's on her third husband and both of the other two died under suspicious circumstances," she explained. "And that hit man could have been Harold Haggard."

"I'm going to the FBI tomorrow and tell them about the airplane and what I saw even if I wind up getting egg on my face," Boulder said. "They will have jurisdiction if an aircraft is involved. That plane should be searched. We have enough to know that something is going to happen on First Thursday."

They continued around the trail, discussing aspects of the case. They agreed that there were just too many unanswered questions. Eventually they arrived back where they started, their cars waiting above like horses tied to a fence.

"I'll call you after I meet with the FBI," Boulder said. They paused and looked at each other face-to-face. There was a respect between them. Maybe something else.

Then from behind a tree came a voice that Boulder had heard before. "I wouldn't count on going to the FBI if I were you."

Even in the dim light they could tell immediately that it was Harold Haggard. The dim light glistened from his shaved head and reflected a gleam from the massive .357 magnum he held in his right hand.

"Are you going to do the same thing to us you did to Randy Crowley?" Boulder asked.

"I'm not going to do anything to you," Haggard said. "You are going to do it to yourselves." Boulder and

Officer Worthmore turned heads toward each other. "You may begin by throwing your guns on the ground beside me. Right now!" he demanded.

Worthmore slowly pulled up her khaki shirt, withdrew her police-issued weapon and did as instructed. Boulder reached down and removed the snub-nosed revolver from his ankle holster and tossed it at Haggard's feet. Haggard reached down and picked up Boulder's pistol and then placed the .357 back in his holster. He raised Boulder's gun and pointed it at Officer Worthmore.

"You seem to have a plan," Boulder said.

"There is no doubt about it," Haggard said. "Officer found shot to death with private investigator's gun and private investigator shot to death with officer's gun. And in Saucier Park no less. This will certainly give people something to talk about."

"Before you carry out your plan, would you like to tell us about Crowley?" Boulder asked.

"Of course," Haggard said. "He was merely collateral damage. Got into places he shouldn't have been and told people he shouldn't have told."

"What should he not have told?" Boulder asked.

"That a foolproof little plan was about to unfold that was going to make some people very rich," said Haggard.

"One of them being you," Worthmore said.

"Of course. You don't think I would participate in

something unless the stakes were high, do you? That is what makes me who I am," answered Haggard.

"How high are the stakes?" Boulder asked.

"Let's see. There are twelve of them. Ten have $2 million each on them, and the pilots have $1.5 million each. You do the math," said Haggard.

"That's $23 million!" Officer Worthmore said.

"It's very simple," said Haggard. "The plane goes down. The insurance pays off. Everybody lives happily ever after."

"So Randy Crowley stumbled on your little plan and you just killed him," Boulder said.

"What else could I do? And then you came along that night and made it so much easier. I was afraid that some baseball mom with a load of kiddie leaguers would be the first to arrive on the scene. But you, Mr. Jack Boulder, you did your part so well. I thank you."

"How did you know Crowley would be there at the right time?" Boulder asked.

"It was simple. I just called him on the telephone and told him that I found a laptop computer at the park that appeared to be his. Of course I stole it from his car earlier in the evening. Do you know how easy it is to open a car door?"

"Can't say as I do," Boulder replied.

"Now you two are giving me another opportunity. It will look like the murder suspect drew a gun on the cop, who had to shoot, et cetera, et cetera. With two bodies and two guns it will be easy to figure out. And now Worthmore you can kiss this . . ."

Suddenly, a horn started blowing and lights started going off and in the parking lot behind them. Boulder seized the moment and lunged at Haggard, but not in time to stop the gun from exploding in his left ear as his head plowed into Haggard's stomach. The bullet hit Officer Pat Worthmore in the center of the chest and she fell backward. Boulder and Haggard crashed to the ground. Boulder grabbed the gun with his left hand and smashed his right hand into Haggard's face. Haggard rolled over on top of Boulder and the gun went off again, this time firing into the dirt underneath them as they rolled over and over.

In the background the horns and lights were still sounding. Haggard kneed Boulder in the midsection, causing two ribs to break. Boulder doubled up in pain. Haggard pulled his gun from his holster, got to his knees and aimed the massive .357 magnum at Boulder' head. As he began to squeeze the trigger a crack was heard from behind him. Haggard rolled his eyes upward into his head as his mouth opened. As he died, he tumbled forward onto Jack Boulder.

The weight of Haggard, coupled with his injured ribs, was all Boulder could take. Just before he lost consciousness, Boulder looked up to see Laura Webster standing beside his Camaro, the horn and lights still pulsating on and off. She was using her set of keys to his car and had activated the alarm system. He then turned to see Officer Pat Worthmore standing there holding a .25 caliber pistol in her right hand, a small puff of smoke coming from its barrel.

Laura ran to Boulder. As she clutched him, she tossed her extra set of keys to the Camaro to Officer Worthmore and said, "Would you see if you can turn that thing off?"

Worthmore took the key set and pointed it toward the car and punched the "panic" button twice. The Camaro became quiet again.

"You got here just in time," Officer Worthmore said.

"After I thought about all that Jack told me tonight, I knew something bad was about to happen so I drove up here as fast as I could," Laura explained. "He told me you were meeting him at the police department at the end of your shift. I went there, but they said you were already gone. As I was pulling out, I saw Jack's car over here. It was pure luck. That's all."

"Maybe so. Maybe not."

"Don't you believe in luck?" Laura asked.

"I believe in preparation. A small caliber pistol in an ankle holster and a bullet-proof vest are what I call luck."

EPILOGUE

Later that night the FBI removed a bomb from the SVN Tech jet. It had a timing device set to go off shortly after the scheduled takeoff on Friday morning.

• • •

Ed McGreely was arrested for conspiracy to commit murder and insurance fraud. He later pled guilty and was sentenced to twelve consecutive prison terms.

Officer Pat Worthmore was soon promoted to Sargeant and remains on the Southaven Police Department.

Carson Kelly opened a new computer store in Memphis.

Jefferson Stallman recovered from heart surgery and was last seen fishing in the Caribbean with a U. S. Senator from Tennessee.

Melinda Craft was late for work because her son, Adam, became ill at school. She still attends baseball games at Snowden Grove Park.

Jack Boulder spent a day in the hospital and he and Laura Webster returned to Jackson. Each went back to their chosen vocations. They have had no further marriage discussions.